COURAGE, TEARS, AND THE GLORY

The Immigrant Who Defied the Wind

PAUL HAN

PAUL HAN
Published by Paul Han

Printed Worldwide
First Printing 2025
First Edition 2025

ISBN: 979-8-9930214-0-9

Library of Congress Control Number: 2025920343

10 9 8 7 6 5 4 3 2 1

For rights and permissions:
Divine America Media Inc.
Email: paul@divineamerica.com

COURAGE, TEARS, AND THE GLORY

TABLE OF CONTENTS

DEDICATION

To my beloved wife, Jean —
It was 53 years ago when I met a brilliant 18-year-old violinist, a first-year instrumental music student. Since that day, we have journeyed together through a life full of tears and laughter, hand in hand.

Together, we raised our two loving daughters, Esther and Lisa, and watched them grow with joy and pride. And now, we are blessed with five beautiful grandchildren
— Dean, Luke, Devin, Olivia, and Sophie
— each nurtured with your unwavering love and devotion.

This book is dedicated to you, Jean —
my partner in every season,
my greatest blessing,
and the music of my life.

Paul
Summer of 2025

PREFACE

We all carry storms within us. Some are born of loss. Others of betrayal.

And sometimes, they're simply the winds of time, uprooting everything we thought was safe.

In *Courage, Tears, and Glory: The Immigrant Who Defied the Wind,* you will walk beside Taejun Kang, a man who stood at the gates of a foreign land with nothing but a suitcase, a crying child, and a heart determined to survive.

This is not the story of overnight success. It is a long, hard road marked by hunger, rejection, sweat, and sleepless nights. But within that journey are also the quiet moments of hope: a kind neighbor offering a mattress, an unexpected payment that puts food on the table, and a child's voice whispering, "I like our home."

What you are about to read is fiction rooted in truth. Though names and scenes have been shaped for narrative flow, the heart of this novel is drawn from the real struggles of immigrants who arrived empty-handed and left a legacy, of families who sacrificed silently so the next generation could dream loudly.

This book is for anyone who has ever questioned whether they'd make it. It's also for those who've had doors slammed, but still kept knocking. In addition, it's for every person who has ever whispered, even in their darkest hour: "It's not over yet."

May this story give you courage, permission to cry, and a glimpse of glory.

— *Paul Han*

CHAPTER 1

EXODUS

"The engine caught fire." Silence fell over the cabin. Just moments ago, the air had been filled with quiet conversations and clinking coffee cups. But now, even the flight attendants' breathing could be heard.

Taejun gripped the armrest tightly.

The captain's voice echoed through the speaker.

"Ladies and gentlemen, due to an engine malfunction, we will attempt an emergency landing. Once again, we ask for your full cooperation."

A flight from New York to London. Taejun closed his eyes. And in that moment, he recalled a day long ago—his departure from Narita Airport. It had been the same then.

It was the evening of January 4, 1982, at Narita Airport in Tokyo. Taejun stood at the gate, clutching a worn briefcase.

In his hand was a currency exchange receipt for $183. That was all the money he had.

Just like now, as flames rose from the engine, back then too, Taejun stood at the edge of a cliff in life. But he had survived. And he would survive again.

~ ~ ~

The departure lounge at Narita Airport was bustling with passengers awaiting their evening flights. Through the darkening windows, the runway lights shimmered faintly, and boarding announcements flowed steadily over the speakers.

Taejun stood quietly, gazing out from one corner of the airport.

His father silently looked at Taejun, Yujin, and Minseo. No words were exchanged. They had already spoken at length during the past few months in Tokyo. There was nothing more to say. They knew what needed to be done.

During those months, they had stayed together in Aoyama, exploring parts of Japan, while his father had calmly shared the ups and downs of his life and business. A few months earlier, Taejun's father had been running a clothing business in Korea. But that past summer, burdened by bank loans and private debt, he lost his factories, his company—everything.

He had come to Tokyo, searching for another chance.

Taejun had witnessed his father's downfall. Although his own business was separate, it convinced him that Korea's business environment was too harsh. And so, he decided to go to America. He was somewhat familiar with the country. Taejun had visited New York and San Francisco multiple times for trade meetings over the years.

~ ~ ~

Before Taejun's departure, his father quietly handed him 20,000 yen. It was what remained after purchasing one-way tickets for the three of them, as he had been unable to collect outstanding payments during the year-end. That was Taejun's entire fortune for his journey to America.

As boarding time approached, Taejun bowed deeply to his father and said, "Goodbye." It was a short but deeply meaningful farewell. His father stood silently, watching him. He neither waved nor said another word. Taejun led Yujin and Minseo toward the boarding gate.

His steps were firm, but his mind was heavy.

As the plane roared down the runway and lifted into the sky, Taejun looked out the window.

The city lights grew smaller, disappearing into the endless darkness. Yujin, holding Minseo in her arms, had fallen asleep. But Taejun couldn't close his eyes for a second. This journey to America was not a mere relocation—it was a new beginning and a leap into an uncertain future.

Yujin majored in violin at university, played in orchestras, and taught children. But America was unfamiliar territory. Though she had followed the path Taejun chose, she couldn't shake her anxiety about this new environment.

After five hours, the plane landed at Honolulu Airport in Hawaii. Taejun, holding only one-way tickets, worried there might be trouble at immigration. Fortunately, with a small child, the process went smoothly. As he gathered their luggage, the reality of arriving in America slowly began to sink in. But still, all he had in hand was $183.

~ ~ ~

From Honolulu, they flew to Los Angeles. There, Yujin's friend Minkyung's husband, Kevin and Taejun's younger brother, Taesoo greeted them. Though Taejun and Kevin were not well acquainted, Kevin had driven a large van to pick up his wife's friend.

"You must be tired from the long trip."

After a brief exchange of greetings, Taejun nodded silently. It had been a long journey, but it was far from over. They left the airport and headed straight to Minkyung's house in Long Beach. The passing cityscape felt unfamiliar to Taejun. Though he had traveled to New York and San Francisco multiple times for business, this time was different. This was not just another business trip. This was where his new life would begin.

Arriving in Long Beach, Minkyung welcomed them warmly. She and Yujin quickly fell into conversation, laughter flowing easily as they reunited after a long time. Taejun sat quietly, listening, thinking of the belongings they had brought:

- Yujin's violin
- A few family photo albums
- Two red mink blankets
- A single-person electric rice cooker from Japan
- A few of Yujin's music sheets
- Several winter clothes for each of them

That was everything.

Soon after, they moved to Yujin's aunt's house in Irvine. It was a quiet home with a small garden visible through the window. The house was warm inside, but Taejun did not unpack.

Their place to stay had not been decided yet.

He gazed out the window, lost in thought, and asked himself, *What will I do?*

He planned to continue working in trade, but nothing was set in stone. One thing was clear—there was no longer any hope left in Korea, and he would have to find his future in America. He knew all too well that in his hands were that $183 and the future he would have to build with his own two hands.

Chapter 2

First Night in Long Beach

Fifteen days after arriving in the U.S., with help from his younger brother Taesoo, they rented a small apartment along Anaheim Street in Long Beach. It had two bedrooms, and it seemed like many Korean families lived in the building. The apartment was old, but that wasn't what mattered to them right now. It had a roof, a lock on the door, and a place to sleep. That was enough.

On their first night, rain fell over the Long Beach sky. Raindrops pounded against the windows, and the sound of rain hitting the neighboring factory's roof didn't stop all night. Whenever the wind blew, the worn-out windows shook, and the cold air seeping through the cracks made the room even colder.

Taejun couldn't fall asleep easily. They laid a mink blanket over the carpeted floor, and the three of them shared the other one to cover themselves. There were no pillows, so Taejun folded a phone book to rest his head on. It was hard and uncomfortable, but this wasn't the time to complain.

Next to him, Yujin and Minseo also struggled to sleep. Minseo whimpered in her sleep but soon calmed down in Yujin's arms. Taejun stared at the ceiling, lost in thought.

Can I really do this?

He had left everything behind in Korea. There was nowhere to return to, no room to start over. He had to endure as long as he could and find a way forward.

Outside, cars splashed through puddles, and the sound of rain continued to wrap around the room. By morning, the rain had stopped, but the air was still cold. Yujin took Minseo and headed out to find a nearby supermarket. Minseo held tightly onto Yujin's hand, looking around curiously at the unfamiliar streets. The buildings, roads, and cars—everything was different from Korea. It was Yujin's first time in America. The streets were wide, and the parking lots in front of the stores were packed with cars.

As they entered the supermarket, the air was filled with unfamiliar smells and unfamiliar products. Yujin grabbed a shopping basket and slowly walked around the aisles. Familiar Korean ingredients were nowhere to be seen. Everything was new.

She carefully studied the price tags for a long time. They didn't have much money. She placed a few onions, a pack of rice, sausages, a carton of milk, and one bag of snacks for Minseo into the basket. Every item was chosen with care.

"Eleven dollars and sixty cents," the cashier said with a bright smile. Yujin awkwardly pulled money from her wallet and handed it over.

Taking the change, she once again held Minseo's hand tightly. On the way back home, Minseo clutched the milk carton in one hand.

Back at the apartment, Taejun had pulled out his old single-serving rice cooker from Japan, a small appliance used during business trips.

"The rice cooker still works," Taejun said.

With no dining table, they flipped over a box of Ichiban ramen to make a makeshift table. Taejun grilled the sausages in a frying pan, scooped out freshly cooked rice from the small rice cooker, and the three of them sat down around their humble meal.

Then, the sound of a neighbor's door opening echoed. The door opened, and a middle-aged Korean woman dragged out a small single-size mattress.

As Yujin looked at it, the woman said, "My youngest used to sleep on this, but we don't need it anymore. If you want it, you can have it."

Yujin hesitated for a moment. But it was better than sleeping on the floor. "Thank you so much," she said.

She carefully brought the mattress inside. It had a few stains from bed-wetting, but even that was better than sleeping directly on the floor. That night, Yujin and Minseo slept on the small mattress under the red mink blanket. The dim streetlight outside faintly lit up the room.

Taejun quietly watched them and wondered, *What kind of life will we build here?*

Outside the window, the wind gently brushed past.

CHAPTER 3

REMINISCENCE

2025, Downtown Los Angeles.

Chairman Kang Taejun stood by the window of his office, quietly gazing toward LAX. In the distance, planes rose and descended in a repetitive rhythm. On his desk rested the *Immigrant Business Leadership Award* trophy he had recently received. Beside it lay a commemorative booklet from the event.

Taejun opened the booklet. On the very first page was a black-and-white photograph from 1982.

It was an image created on January 19, 1982, at a small apartment in Long Beach.

Taejun, his wife Yujin, and their young daughter Minseo sat on the floor sharing a meal.

He stared at the photo. In that moment, long-buried memories slowly began to surface.

January 1982, Long Beach.

It was a rainy night. The sound of rain tapping on factory rooftops echoed vividly through the window. The room was dark and silent.

Taejun looked down at the ramen box on the floor. On it sat freshly cooked rice and a few sausages. It was too humble to be called a dining table, but it was all they had.

He gazed at the scene, etching it deep into his heart. *Never forget this moment.* That single meal wasn't just food. It was a vow to survive and a symbol of a new beginning.

"Chairman, your next meeting is about to start."

His secretary's voice interrupted. Taejun quietly closed the booklet and returned to his seat. But in his mind, that night lingered—the rainy evening, a meal with his wife and daughter.

That was the man he once was. And because of him, he is who he is today.

Taejun drove toward the Beverly Hills Hilton. As he passed the towering mixed-use buildings on Wilshire Boulevard, he suddenly recalled an early memory—the apartment manager interview back when they had just arrived in America. It had been barely two months since they immigrated.

In a corner of their apartment, he installed a Western Union Telex. He also opened a P.O. Box at the post office. He began reaching out to old clients in the U.S. and companies in Korea, sourcing samples of kitchenware, toys, ceramics, and building materials.

Yujin registered as an international student at the Korean consulate and studied the bus routes around LA. Taejun didn't yet have a driver's license, so his younger brother, Taesoo, drove him everywhere. Before long, it was mid-April. Taejun finally got his license and could move freely on his own.

But life grew harder.

Taesoo's car was a decade-old Oldsmobile with a V8 engine. The broken muffler made it sound like a tank echoing through the neighborhood.

Also, Taesoo's part-time restaurant job couldn't support Taejun's family of three. Taejun began to grow anxious.

He tried selling samples at a flea market. At dawn, they loaded the samples into the trunk and headed out with Yujin and Minseo. Spreading a cloth over the car hood, they laid out ceramics and toys from Taiwan and called out prices—$22 the first day and $26 the next.

After buying Minseo a cola, they were already losing money on the booth fees. Still, Minseo seemed to enjoy watching people in the blazing sun.

Their pockets were empty again, and Taejun went job hunting once more. Eventually, he started a part-time job at a fish market after a neighbor introduced him to the owner. He arrived at dawn, mopped the floors, and did other shop-cleaning chores. When customers arrived, he'd pull out large fish and trim the fins with a knife. The owner would then carefully fillet the rest and hand it to the customers.

But on his second day, the owner said, "Mister, this isn't the kind of job you should be doing. Please look for something else."

She handed him $45 for the two days he worked.

Now, Taejun even felt embarrassed to face Taesoo. They barely spoke. Then one day, Kevin's father, Youngmin, offered to co-sign for him on a TV purchase.

~ ~ ~

On their way to JCPenney, he casually remarked: "You don't have a green card, you've got a kid. It's not easy living like this. Have you considered a sham marriage to send Minseo to her maternal grandparents in Seoul?"

Taejun said nothing.

Taejun was 22 and Yujin was 18. They met through Sujin, the younger sister of Taejun's friend, Minsu. Yujin had long hair flowing below her waist, and she looked beautiful holding a violin.

When Taejun was serving in the military in Gwangju, she once visited him on the pretext of a local recital. At the army headquarters, a call came through from the front gate: "There's a lovely young lady from Seoul holding a violin."

Yujin often sent packages filled with cigarettes, underwear, and snacks with money from her academic scholarships. Taejun's friend, who worked as a censor in the military post office, often opened them first and sneakily took some items.

On payday, Taejun would use most of his 500-won salary to buy a copy of *Women's Central Monthly* magazine and mail it to her.

By June, things had gotten even harder.

One day, Taejun saw a job ad for an apartment manager. It said that managing a 51-unit, 5-story building came with a one-bedroom apartment and $300 a month in salary. He could even do side work if time allowed.

He woke early, drove Taesoo's Oldsmobile onto the 405 and then the 10 freeway. He was nervous. He thought, *If I can get this job, at least we won't have to worry about rent.*"

But the interview ended too quickly.

"If you don't have a green card, we can't let you handle rent checks."

Taejun silently got up and walked out. As he got into the car, his stomach suddenly cramped. Whether it was from the tension or the morning coffee, the urge was overwhelming. He sped off in a panic. But it was still early, and there were no public restrooms like McDonald's in the neighborhood.

Sweat beaded on his forehead. He drove block after block, desperately searching—but there was no way.

Then he spotted an empty round ice cream tub Minseo had left in the backseat. Taejun turned into a quiet alley shaded by trees, parked, and quickly climbed into the back.

What kind of life is this… The car was silent. Taejun let out a long, deep sigh.

CHAPTER 4

LAMENTATION

In early July 1982, Kukje Corporation Manager Lee contacted Taejun.

"Mr. Kang, there's a working glove show at the Long Beach Convention Center. You'll meet people there. It could be a great opportunity."

Countless trade companies were displaying their products at the convention center. Taejun cautiously visited each booth, collecting business cards, greeting people, and gathering product samples. Some booths offered sandwiches and bottled water.

Taejun filled his stomach and connected with even more vendors.

After leaving the hall, he didn't know the bus routes and wanted to save on fare. The sun beat down mercilessly overhead. The heat radiated off the burning asphalt, seeping into the soles of his feet. Sweat didn't just run down his back; it streamed down his face, blurring his vision. His legs grew heavier with each step, and his shoes were soaked with sweat.

He walked for four hours.

By the time he reached home, blisters had formed between his toes, and tears welled in his eyes. *Now… I need to make a decision,* he thought.

A few days later, his friend, Taekyung from Seoul, got in touch with him. "Taejun, my older brother, Taehyun, is in Dallas. He's the branch manager of Far East Trading Company. Maybe if you meet him, he could help you out."

Taejun perked up. After he talked with Taehyun, Taejun contacted Taekyung, told him, "Your brother said I should visit. He's in charge of steel."

Taejun began searching across the U.S. for steel suppliers. Eventually, he was introduced to Michael, a friend of Kevin, who was Min-kyung's husband. Michael was a young and bold entrepreneur. He enjoyed traveling and flying his small plane.

Taejun was eager to supply steel products to Far East Trading.

Taejun headed to Dallas. It felt like his last chance.

One afternoon in August, Taejun visited Michael again. "Far East Trading showed some interest."

Michael jumped with excitement.

"Really? So, we're this close to a multimillion-dollar deal?"

That night, Michael took Taejun to Kevin's Marina Bar for dinner and drinks. There, Michael opened up.

"I want a new partner. If this deal with Far East goes through, we might break into the Korean market too."

At that moment, Taejun carefully—but firmly—spoke up.

"Michael, there's something more important to me than this deal."

"What is it?"

"I need to survive here. Could your company sponsor my green card?"

Michael paused, deep in thought. "I'm not someone who makes decisions like that lightly."

Taejun, tense, clasped his hands together and held his breath.

Then, Michael nodded.

Taejun thought, *This might just change my life.*

He was finally able to receive a green card sponsorship through Michael's company. He worked as a sales manager in charge of the Korean market. Taejun shouted silently in his heart: *Heaven has blessed me!*

On August 31st, it was time to leave the Long Beach apartment. Taesoo's friends came with a car and helped load the trunk with their belongings. Taejun's family would temporarily stay at the home of Min Hyung-bae, who lived in Artesia City.

After loading the last box into the trunk, Taejun closed the door. Before leaving, he took one last look at the shabby apartment. The worn-out door, cracked tiles, and cramped living room. All of it was now in the past. The sky was oddly clear. He let out a deep breath and got back in the car.

That morning, President Min came across a job ad in the newspaper for a Korean-owned dry cleaner.

"Upscale neighborhood near Long Beach Beachfront – Hiring Korean cashier."

President Min called the owner and touted Yujin as a potential hire. "I'll vouch for her," President Min said. "She's a trustworthy person with a university degree from Seoul."

Yujin's first interview was a breeze. She agreed to start in four weeks as a front cashier, working 6 hours a day, 30 hours a week.

Watching from a distance with a jealous eye, Taejun saw that the dry cleaner's owner was elegant, intelligent-looking, and attractive.

After the interview, Yujin said, "There's no other path left. We have to survive."

There was resolve in her eyes.

After the move, they had dinner with President Min and his wife. For the first time in a long while, Taejun's family had a peaceful meal.

That night, they laid out blankets on the wooden floor of a room they didn't usually use.

Taejun lay down with Yujin and Minseo.

The next day was the memorial for President Min's father. The whole family gathered for the ritual and shared a meal. They were family. Taejun's family members were there, but they were outsiders.

After the event ended, Taejun stepped outside. He moved the car to the driveway. As he opened the door and sat in the driver's seat, he slowly placed both hands on the steering wheel. His fingers trembled. This wasn't the life he had dreamed of. But it was the life he had chosen.

As he closed his eyes, every moment from the past few months rushed in at once. Four hours walking under the scorching sun, and Minseo's tiny hand. At that moment, he could hold it in no longer.

"Now I'm a man who brought his wife and daughter into someone else's spare room…"

Sobs filled the car.

With his face buried in the steering wheel, he let out everything he had been holding in. And in the darkness, his tears flowed endlessly.

CHAPTER 5

FIRST PAYCHECK AT THE DRY CLEANER

Autumn in California still feels like summer. The sun blazes down intensely, and even the breeze is a little warm. It had already been nine months since Taejun arrived in America.

His life was still tough, but within it, faint sparks of hope were beginning to appear.

Early in the morning, Taejun set out with Yujin and Minseo in the car. He dropped Yujin off at the dry cleaner in Belmont Shore in Long Beach and then took Minseo straight to daycare. Belmont Shore was a wealthy, predominantly white neighborhood by the beach, and most customers at the dry cleaner were neatly dressed middle-class or upper-class clients.

But even as Yujin smiled politely at them, she remained constantly anxious. Since she hadn't registered for school, she had been reported to immigration as a no-show. Once her visa expired, she would be at risk of becoming an undocumented immigrant.

The work at the dry cleaner was simple. When customers came in, she turned the clothing rack to find their garments and handled the payments. But even in those simple tasks, her nerves were always on edge. When police officers entered, her heart would drop. She would quietly slip into the restroom or the storage room, afraid they might ask about her status.

The shop owner's nephew, who was also on a student visa, seemed carefree as he enjoyed hearty lunches. In contrast, Yujin couldn't afford to buy lunch and made do with toast, a few slices of carrot, and an apple from home. There were rows of fast-food places near the shop, but eating there was a luxury she couldn't afford.

After dropping off Minseo, Taejun would spend time at a burger place nearby or by the beach. At 2:30 in the afternoon, he would pick up Minseo and head to Yujin's dry cleaner.

On her first day at daycare, Minseo wet her pants. When Taejun came to pick her up, the assistant handed him a plastic bag with her wet clothes and said Minseo had cried a lot. Minseo had cried out, "Appa, Appa (Daddy)," but the staff misheard it as "Apple" and gave her a piece of fruit. From that day, Taejun taught her a few English words: "Water," "Toilet," and "Daddy."

Thankfully, the daycare was a government-supported facility for low-income families, so there was no fee, and they provided free lunch and snacks.

Taejun drove a car that Taesoo helped him obtain for $550. The car was like a ticking time bomb. It could break down at any moment. The engine roared loudly whenever it started, and the gas gauge was broken, so he had to refuel based on instinct. He was always nervous the fuel might run out unexpectedly.

He was gradually getting used to living at Mr. Min's house. Still, he felt he was imposing. He knew he couldn't stay there forever. Taejun was struggling every day, shuttling between the dry cleaner and daycare, just to keep things afloat

He chased down every opportunity that came his way — steel supply, construction materials, and hotel goods among them. He needed to apply for a visa extension and prepare documents for a work permit. The lawyer's fee was a burden, but he held on to hope that if he delivered products to Far East Trading, he might receive a commission from Michael.

Finally, Yujin received her first weekly paycheck from the dry cleaner—$160 for her $5-per hour. But the joy of holding that money in her hand was indescribable.

That evening, Taejun, Yujin, and Minseo went to Jack in the Box. They ordered two burgers and one soda. They asked for a water cup, and the three of them shared everything.

They weren't full, but it was the happiest meal they'd had in a long time.

After finishing her shift at the dry cleaner, Yujin began teaching violin lessons. By teaching two kids for an hour each, she could earn a little extra income outside her regular pay. On lesson days, Taejun would walk around the neighborhood with Minseo. Sometimes, they used the bathroom at McDonald's. Holding Minseo's tiny hand, Taejun sang children's songs.

"When Mom goes to the island to gather oysters~" Minseo sang along, her pronunciation clumsy, but it moved Taejun deeply.

By mid-October, a ray of light was beginning to shine into Taejun's life. He submitted the paperwork for a work permit to the lawyer's office, and he was able to cover the $1,000 retainer by borrowing money from Yujin's aunt. The road ahead was still long, but at least they had taken the first step forward.

And finally, they signed a lease for a small one-bedroom apartment. It was only possible because Yujin's friend, Minkyung, co-signed for them. Rent was $385 a month, including water, but they had to pay separately for electricity and gas. It was a small apartment complex with just seven households in a two-story building, and Taejun's unit was No. 7, at the far end of the second floor.

There was no furniture, so they slept on mink blankets spread out on the floor and pulled one over themselves. But it was different from before. This was no longer just a fight for survival.

Taejun was preparing for real life—right here.

One night, Minseo lay between Taejun and Yujin, gently stroking her mother's face with her small hand. She whispered:

"Mom, Dad... I love our home."

At that, Taejun and Yujin looked at each other and smiled. They had nothing but now, at least, they had a shared dream.

CHAPTER 6

WORK PERMIT

It was now November. Yujin's college friend from Seoul, Kyung-mi, had come to LA to perform with the Seoul Philharmonic Orchestra. Yujin herself had once been a member.

They met for dinner at the Ambassador Hotel in LA. Over a pleasant meal, Kyung-mi handed over several gifts that Yujin's mother had sent from home.

On their way home late at night, while driving down the 110 freeway, the car suddenly began to sputter, as if the engine was about to stall. The gas gauge had been broken for some time, so they had been estimating when to fill up based on intuition. Though it had usually worked out fine, tonight was different. The engine began to die.

Unable to steer toward the outer lane, they barely managed to pull over onto the narrow inside shoulder. After a few tense minutes, Taejun turned the key, and thankfully, the engine started again.

It was past midnight. Cars were speeding by in all directions. In the backseat, Minseo gripped Yujin's hand tightly, her face filled with fear. When there was a break in traffic, Taejun carefully merged back onto the road. Somehow, they made it home safely, having survived what felt like a terrifying brush with danger.

It was a moment they would never forget.

~ ~ ~

It was July. Taejun's family had been living in the States for seven months. All the paperwork for the work permit had finally been submitted. Looking back on the year that had passed, Taejun felt a flood of emotion. What kind of life awaited them in the new year? Excitement and anxiety collided in his mind.

Each morning began with taking Yujin to the dry cleaners, then washing and dressing Minseo, feeding her breakfast, getting her ready, and dropping her off at daycare before Taejun started his work.

Without a proper means of communication, he had to rely solely on phone calls and occasionally send samples via DHL.

One afternoon, Taejun received a call from Attorney Miller. His work permit had been approved.

Tears welled up in his eyes. "We're going to be okay now," he said to himself. *We can finally live here. The three of us—together.*

It was overwhelming.

He picked up a still-napping Minseo from daycare, then waited for Yujin in the dry cleaner's parking lot. As soon as she stepped into the car after her shift, he blurted out the news. Yujin burst into tears. What a precious, long-awaited moment it was.

In the past, whenever a police officer came into the store, she would quietly slip into the storage room or the restroom. But now… she had a way forward.

That evening, the three of them went to McDonald's on Anaheim Street. They ordered cheeseburgers, Filet-O-Fish, and French fries—a modest but joyful celebration. *Finally*, they could live in this country without fear. And maybe, someday, even visit Korea again.

~ ~ ~

Time passed, and it was now September.

The steel supply deal with Far East Trading was going smoothly. It had already been over two years since Taejun began working with Michael. Now that his green card application was underway, he was thinking about spending another year in the steel business, then maybe transitioning into the computer industry. He discussed the idea openly, though he promised to continue helping Far East Trading with their steel orders even after the change.

With the green card application process now in motion, he meticulously prepared all necessary documents and sent them, along with a $1,050 fee, to the lawyer's office.

All that was left was to wait for the interview date.

CHAPTER 7

PERMANENT RESIDENCY AND A NEW BEGINNING

The new year of 1984, filled with hope and ambition, had already begun with passion. Taejun was carrying out his New Year's plans while requesting documents such as a certificate of personal records and military status confirmation from Korea to apply for permanent residency. He was also in close communication with his attorney's office.

Meanwhile, Taejun's family prepared the required documents —photos, passport copies, fingerprint forms—for the three of them and sent them to Attorney Miller, submitting them for the permanent residency interview. At last, they received their interview date.

Ah, what a deeply moving moment!

"This year, our family will finally take root in this land."

Taejun imagined himself as a tiger with wings. But suddenly, an unexpected crisis struck.

During his medical exam, a positive reaction appeared on his left arm to the tuberculosis test (tuberculin) he had received when he enlisted in the Korean military. The nurse explained that although he wasn't infected, sometimes people still react to it if the agent remains dormant in the body.

"TB is considered critical by immigration," the nurse said.

Her voice echoed in Taejun's mind. Taejun felt like he couldn't breathe.

"To think this might cancel our green card interview…!"

For the next three or four days, Taejun carefully avoided moving his arm or getting it wet, doing everything he could to prevent a reaction during the retest. This was a matter of fate.

Thankfully, the retest showed no reaction. Taejun breathed a sigh of relief.

"Dear God, please help us."

He couldn't sleep a wink that night. At 5:30 a.m., Taejun got up and woke his family. They quickly dressed, packed some bottled water and light snacks into the car, and left a little after 6 a.m. They parked near the immigration office and ate a quick breakfast in the car.

Yujin turned to Minseo and said, "Minseo, today is a very important day. Shall we say a prayer?"

Around 7 a.m., they arrived at the building and found a long line already stretching far outside. The crowd was divided into two lines—one for general immigration services, and another, with no wait, for green card and citizenship interviews. The family entered the latter and went up to the sixth floor to wait for Miller.

At about 7:30, Attorney Miller approached, waving warmly. He felt like an angel descending from the sky. Just after 8 a.m., their names were called. With tense expressions, they sat down at the interview table, where an officer came out and began reviewing the documents with the attorney. Taejun felt like he was suffocating. Never in his life had he felt such intense anxiety.

More than 30 minutes passed. The three of them stared fixedly in one direction, watching the officer flip through their papers with an unreadable expression. Taejun held his breath.

And finally, the immigration officer said, "Okay, good job! Congratulations, Mr. Kang."

The officer stamped their passports with a satisfying "thump" and returned them.

How could he even begin to express the joy of this moment?

"At last, our family can finally live freely in this country."

They took the elevator down, thanked Attorney Miller several times, and headed back to the parking lot. In the car, the three of them held hands and shouted a loud, joyful "Yahoo!" Taejun drove toward Little Tokyo, and with a beaming smile, they stopped by a tiny soba shop they had visited before. They ordered udon and tonkatsu, and with smiles still on their faces, drove back home to Long Beach.

To think that their family could now live safely in this country. It felt like a dream.

~ ~ ~

Yujin had applied for a work permit, and now she was three months pregnant. She had decided to quit working at the dry cleaner and focus only on teaching lessons to children. Thanks to the owner's kindness, she had worked there for about two years.

Taejun felt endlessly grateful to Yujin for enduring such hard times. A woman who graduated from a top university in Korea and used to perform with an orchestra was now folding strangers' laundry at a dry cleaner, and sometimes even handling their underwear. But she patiently endured it all, trusting that better days would come.

Taejun felt guilt and sorrow. He thought, *I really am such a lousy husband. I brought her here, to a place where we had no one, and made her suffer like this.*

~ ~ ~

Now, Taejun was ready to dream big.

Rather than dealing in hotel supplies or steel products, he envisioned working in a larger global multinational company where he could expand his horizons, learn how large companies operate, and eventually do business across Asia, or even the world. He made up his mind to change the course of his life.

On a sunny morning in Long Beach, Taejun got into a taxi heading to LAX, carrying a small travel bag and a Samsonite suitcase. He hugged Yujin, Minseo, and the unborn baby inside Yujin's belly, pressing their cheeks together with a smile, and said goodbye.

This was Taejun's first business trip to Seoul as an employee of Codeva.

Korean Air Flight 018 to Seoul's Gimpo Airport was fully booked.

How long had it been?

Was this a triumphant return?

Overcome with emotion, Taejun sank into his seat.

He had traveled to Tokyo, New York, San Francisco, and other cities before, but this trip was different. It wasn't just a small trading business anymore. Now, he was representing an American company. And this wasn't general trade; it was in the computer sector, which required expertise.

"Now I must stand on my own as the Korean representative of a multinational company."

Would it go well?

He planned to stay in Seoul for three to four months, build a strong network with 30 to 40 clients, and hit the year's sales targets. If successful, the company might even establish a Korean branch.

Clients responded positively to the fact that a Korean speaker was now in charge of Korea.

The travel budget, including hotel, transportation, meals, and entertainment, was $78 per day. Each meal could not exceed $21 per person.

It was tough.

In Korea, business didn't happen without proper hospitality. One day, while having dinner with a major client, Taejun worried he might go over budget. But all he could order was a $21 dinner.

Time flew by, and by the end of November, Taejun returned to the U.S. with great results. Sales in the first year exceeded expectations, reaching over $5 million. The company seemed satisfied.

But Taejun's actual income was modest. He had signed the employment contract without asking for a high salary, hoping that a Korean branch would be established the following year.

A greater vision was already forming in his mind.

"I'm not just a merchant. I'll become a global businessman overseeing all of Asia."

As the year came to a close, the only thing left was to make a dazzling debut as the head of the Korea branch in the new year.

Yujin, now about a month away from giving birth, was feeling heavy and tired.

But with a new family member on the way, a likely increase in Taejun's salary, and a future full of hope, they could now move forward with renewed purpose. All of this was thanks to Yujin, who endured everything, and their little daughter, Minseo.

CHAPTER 8

BETRAYAL

In the hopeful dawn of the new year, 1985, a new life was born into Taejun's family — David. Everything now seemed to be going smoothly, as if success was laid out before them.

Taejun's family was full of hope and optimism.

Taejun was about to become busier as the head of sales for Codeva Korea. Yujin focused on raising Minseo and David, and Minseo had now adjusted well to daycare. Once the company's health insurance plan kicked in after a 90-day grace period, starting April 1st, they would be covered. Though the salary wasn't large, it was more than what Yujin had been earning at the laundromat, so life was expected to become more comfortable.

Taejun carefully reviewed the employment contract sent from headquarters. Given their current circumstances, all the terms seemed satisfactory, enough for a family of four to get by: An annual salary of $18,000, travel expenses covered, group health insurance, and even a bonus plan.

They agreed to establish a Korean branch office by year's end or early next year. Taejun signed the updated employment agreement and mailed it back.

He spent the early days of the year calling each of the 30 Korean clients he had built relationships with the previous year, extending New Year's greetings and checking whether their budgets would increase. He was busy, but excited. He was ready to fully commit to expanding Codeva's computer business in Korea and dreamed of opening the branch office in the second half of the year.

In February, the company requested a travel budget plan, so Taejun immersed himself in that work. He explained Korea's unique business culture to headquarters and asked for an increased budget for client entertainment expenses. Since the VP of overseas business, Hamilton, was his direct supervisor, Taejun made a heartfelt plea for understanding.

But during a call regarding the budget, an unexpected issue arose.

The U.S. company policy capped meal expenses at $21 per person for an entertainment dinner—roughly ₩20,000 in Korean won—with no exceptions. That meant hotel, meals, transportation, and entertainment all had to be covered with just $78 a day. Even with budget hotels, accommodations alone would cost ₩50,000.

That left only about ₩30,000 to cover meals, travel, and entertaining clients. It was an impossible ask.

Laughing, Taejun joked: "Then I guess I'll have to sleep in the waiting room at Seoul Station like a homeless man."

But the budget negotiation fell apart.

CHAPTER 9

TERMINATION AND DESPAIR

Two days later, Taejun returned home from an outing to find a fax waiting for him from headquarters. The message was simple and curt: the termination of his employment contract.

Taejun couldn't understand what was happening. The next morning, he called the head office.

"You're fired," said the vice president's secretary.

Taejun didn't understand. It was the first time he had ever heard that phrase.

He asked again, hoping he had misheard.

Taejun was in shock. What had gone wrong? He couldn't think of a single reason for this sudden dismissal.

All their plans were now in ruins. They had planned to spend 3 to 4 months in Seoul, build a $5 million business, open a branch office, and finally settle into a comfortable life. But now, without explanation, he had been fired. Yujin and the entire family were devastated.

Thinking back, he realized his joke about sleeping at Seoul Station due to the tight budget must have offended Vice President Hamilton. Taejun felt sure that this was the true reason for his termination.

Unbelievable.

"Or is there some other hidden reason?"

He had heard that in the U.S., an employer could fire an employee at any time, and an employee could leave freely at any time. But this went beyond common sense.

The next day, he called again, explained his situation, and practically begged to stay on — especially now, with a newborn child — but it was no use.

A few days later, he tried calling once more. This time, they asked if his family could return to Korea, as the company now preferred to hire someone residing locally.

It all became clear. The company had already established a $5 million foothold in Korea. By hiring a local Korean resident, they could save tens of thousands of dollars in annual travel expenses and wouldn't need to provide health insurance. It made perfect financial sense for the company.

Taejun could no longer bring himself to beg for the job again.

Despair settled in. "This is betrayal. This is fraud!" Taejun clenched his teeth.

~ ~ ~

All their plans had collapsed. His heart burned with rage and resentment. It felt like he was cornered, like an Egyptian soldier giving chase, with the Red Sea blocking the path forward. His previous ventures in the steel and hotel supply businesses had dried up. He had nothing left to restart. There wasn't much cash on hand either. He sat on the sand at Long Beach, eyes closed.

Where should I go now? And how will I repay this betrayal? The fire of vengeance blazed in his eyes. He clenched his fists and stood up.

Should he dismiss this as just another hardship faced by an immigrant with nothing? He thought he had overcome the worst, but once again he found himself standing at the edge of a cliff. He felt nothing but frustration and guilt, especially toward Yujin.

Determined, Taejun decided to reconnect with every company he had previously done business with. He also wrote and sent out countless résumés.

One day, he tracked down the name of the head of international operations at *Nexora*, a global multinational computer company headquartered in New York. He called their office, but was told that the VP of HR, Jennifer, was away on a business trip and that he should try again later. For now, he sent his résumé, feeling at least somewhat relieved that he had made contact.

About two weeks later, he received a reply. They said that since Nexora had no solid track record or business ties in Korea yet, there were no plans to hire anyone for the Korea position at that time.

Meanwhile, Codeva had already finalized his termination and now informed him by mail that they would not be paying the two months' worth of back wages they owed.

April passed.

Taejun contacted Nexora again. This time, they told him to send a proposal along with any reference materials or sales results from his previous company. So, he prepared a report outlining his achievements and forwarded it along with the proposal.

He applied for unemployment benefits with the EDD, hoping to receive at least a meager amount.

He also sought out a labor law attorney and met with a lawyer named Thompson to consult about the possibility of wrongful termination. However, the attorney fees weren't cheap, and most importantly, he explained that winning a case against a multinational corporation — especially one incorporated in another state — was nearly impossible.

"It would be like David versus Goliath," the lawyer said.

Taejun decided to let it go. As an immigrant with no power, no experience, and no legal knowledge, this was yet another harsh reality he had to accept.

Chapter 10

A New Connection

One morning, the fax machine whirred to life. Taejun checked the paper and saw a message from Nexora's Vice President of International Operations. He was on a business trip to LA and asked if they could meet briefly at the airport.

The next day at noon, Taejun met Dennis at the lobby of the Airport Hyatt Hotel. From the very beginning, Dennis's questions revealed him to be a sharp businessman. Why had Taejun left Codeva?

How much business had he handled? He asked detailed, probing questions without pause.

Taejun barely had a moment to breathe, doing his best to follow along.

It felt like a man hanging off a cliff, desperately reaching for a rope.

After about 30 minutes of intense questioning, Dennis said, "Send me a marketing plan. I'll take a look."

And he suggested they follow up in mid-June. It was just a thread of hope, but Taejun had found a potential connection—and that was something.

But if this didn't work out, he couldn't afford to sit idle any longer. He thought, *Even if I have to work as a janitor, I'll need a decent car to get around.* So, he bought the cheapest car he could find—a Nissan Sentra—and prepared himself to clean buildings if it came to that.

From a branch manager in Korea… to a night janitor in LA. Then, in mid-June, a call came from Nexora. They asked Taejun to visit the New York headquarters on July 1st for an interview with President Patterson. He was also told that sometime in July, he should fly to Japan to meet with the company's head of Asian operations.

"Is the sun finally rising again?"

Taejun's heart pounded so hard, it felt like it would tear apart. If he had another chance…

The thought alone ignited a burning flame of vengeance inside him. He couldn't sleep. The past five months had been absolute hell, a time of total despair. The mix of hope and worry on Yujin and Minseo's faces made him ache inside.

~ ~ ~

On the morning of July 1st, Taejun boarded American Airlines Flight #102 at 8:45 a.m., bound for New York. He was burning with determination and was fueled by vengeance.

The next morning, Taejun stood in front of the Nexora building. A towering skyscraper, at least 50 stories high, loomed above him. Its massive presence made him shrink inside.

At the front desk, he told the receptionist that he had a 9 a.m. appointment with Vice President Dennis and President Patterson. The receptionist made a quick call and then pointed toward the elevators.

"Eighteenth floor, that way."

Taejun took a deep breath, adjusted his tie, and looked at himself in the elevator mirror.

He felt like a soldier heading into battle.

At 9:00 a.m., he shook hands with President Patterson and greeted him politely.

Vice President Dennis joined them and briefly summarized Taejun's background and situation.

The meeting progressed smoothly, and Taejun began to feel quietly relieved.

To think — here I am, sitting across from the president of one of the largest companies in the world...

They discussed necessary preparations: supporting documents, the meeting schedule with the Asia director, potential relocation to New York if hired, and references from three former contacts. President Patterson said they would reach a final decision by July 12.

He struck Taejun as an intellectual, the kind of man who had built a world-class company generating billions in annual revenue. Taejun could hardly believe that he might get a second chance in such a prestigious firm.

After leaving Patterson's office, he had a brief follow-up chat with Dennis, sincerely thanked him, and exited the building. From the executive office, a secretary called a taxi for him.

On the way to JFK Airport, Taejun sat in the cab and whispered a tearful prayer.

"Oh God… Thank you."

American Airlines Flight #103 departed New York and landed at LAX at 8:35 that evening.

Color returned to Taejun's face. Hope returned to his heart.

Three days later, late at night, he received a call from Richard, the head of Nexora's Asia division based in Tokyo.

"Congratulations! We've decided to hire you. Let's work hard together."

"Oh God!"

Taejun rushed to wake Yujin, who was still asleep, and shouted in an excited voice: "Yujin! I did it. I got it!"

Yujin, her face filled with emotion, said softly, "You did so well. I'm so proud of you."

Another mountain had been crossed.

CHAPTER 11

THE ART OF NEGOTIATION

On Sunday morning, the warm autumn sunlight streamed through the window. Taejun and Yujin returned home after attending Mass. In the kitchen, Yujin was busy preparing lunch. The knife danced lightly on the cutting board, and a gentle aroma filled the house as the broth simmered in the pot.

Taejun sat on the sofa and unfolded the newspaper. Just then, Minseo arrived with her two daughters.

"Hi, Appa. I just wanted to see you before you leave."

"Hi, Harabuji."

After gaining years of experience at Sysvora, Minseo was now in charge of group finance at Taejun's company.

Taejun embraced his granddaughters and asked, "How's your school?"

The children nodded enthusiastically, "Great!"

Taejun patted Minseo on the shoulder and said, "So, you're even busier than me, now."

He thought of the little girl who once clung to his hand, drowsy-eyed, on her way to daycare. Now, she was playing a key role in business. Time truly flies.

Over lunch, Minseo cautiously asked Taejun, "Appa, is this contract really that important?"

Taejun put down his spoon and answered, "If the deal goes through, we'll secure a stable client for the next three years. But if it fails, we could face a gap of at least a year."

Minseo nodded and said, "You've always taken bold risks. I'm sure you'll succeed again this time."

Taejun smiled faintly. "Hearing you say that gives me strength."

After lunch, Minseo drove Taejun to John Wayne Airport. On the way, Taejun stared out the window, lost in thought. He was scheduled to take AA Flight 1674 at 3:23 PM and arrive at Chicago O'Hare Airport around 9:30 PM.

This business trip carried deep significance for Taejun. It was the final stage of negotiations for a three-year apparel supply deal with Nyx Sports, an agreement he had been working on for months. If successful, it would bring in millions of dollars over three years and mark a major turning point for the company.

An in-flight announcement signaled the landing at O'Hare. After checking into the Downtown Hilton in a pre-booked limousine, Taejun reviewed the final details in preparation for the meeting.

The next day, in the meeting room, Taejun sat across from Harrington, the procurement director of Nyx Sports. This deal, like one from forty years ago, might be swayed by the smallest of margins.

"We need to make a slight adjustment to the price," Harrington said.

Taejun took a deep breath.

The executive tapped his fingers slowly on the table. "Can this price truly guarantee the profit margins we expect?"

Taejun met his gaze firmly. There was no room for hesitation. "Our products can't be judged by cost alone. Consider our on-time delivery, quality, and the performance we've proven over the past five years—this price is the most optimal."

The other side still seemed to hesitate.

But Taejun knew. The key to negotiation was enduring silence.

A tense stillness filled the room.

And finally, the man nodded and said, "Alright. We accept the terms."

Taejun exhaled quietly as he looked at the signed contract. On the way back to the hotel, he suddenly recalled the procurement bid he prepared in Korea over 40 years ago. It was the late 1980s, 3 a.m. in the Lotte Hotel. He vividly remembered analyzing and reviewing the prices.

Facing competition from foreign firms, Taejun made bold decisions. In the end, he won all three contracts, an almost miraculous feat. The price differences were just $1,000, $3,000, and $6,000.

I have to push forward with this price. His mental calculator raced. *Is this right? Or wrong?*

Ultimately, he chose to take the risk, and that decision changed his life.

That small margin led to extraordinary results—contracts worth a total of $2.5 million. It was another turning point in Taejun's life.

After dinner at the hotel, he stopped by the third-floor bar.

He ordered caviar and champagne, then gazed out at the Chicago night skyline. As he took a sip, the smooth bubbles slid down his throat. The city lights outside sparkled more vividly than ever.

He remembered himself forty years ago, alone in a hotel room, wrestling with decisions. So much had changed since then, yet the essence remained the same.

He reflected on the past—and then looked at the present. Life had always been a cycle of challenges and perseverance. But through it all, Taejun had grown stronger, more resilient, and ready to go even farther.

Victory is always decided in a moment of choice. Whether forty years ago or now, he was still standing at the heart of that decision.

And outside the window, the night lights of the city shone even brighter.

CHAPTER 12

BACK TO TOKYO

Taejun wrapped up his schedule in Chicago and returned to California. Leaving behind the chill of Chicago O'Hare Airport, he arrived at John Wayne Airport, where the familiar warmth welcomed him. The stars in the night sky seemed especially bright. As he rode home in the company car waiting at the airport, he finally exhaled a sigh of relief.

The business trip had been a success. By securing a three-year long-term contract with Nyx Sports, he had closed a multi-million-dollar deal. But rather than a sense of achievement, new challenges and tasks filled Taejun's mind.

When he arrived home, Yujin brought him a warm cup of tea. She said, "You must be tired."

With just those few words, the fatigue seemed to melt away.

A few days later, Taejun went to headquarters for a meeting with key executives. With the new contract in place, expanding the business and hiring additional staff had become necessary. Taejun decided to accelerate the company's global market expansion.

"The next five years will determine how far we grow," he said to the boardroom of executives. "We need to aggressively target the Korean and Southeast Asian markets, while solidifying our presence in North America. We should also consider establishing new branches. We could also look into M&A

opportunities and explore collaborations with global brands."

During the meeting, Taejun recalled his younger days with Yujin. From the hardships that began in a humble laundromat, he had risen to lead a global company. But he had no intention of stopping here. He was ready for new goals, greater challenges. That night, Taejun sat in his study and opened his diary.

For over 30 years, he had used the same burgundy leather notebook. It had been by his side through every chapter of his journey, including when he visited Moscow on a business trip on August 18, 1991, during the coup that brought down President Gorbachev.

It was with him when the plane from New York to London caught fire midair and had to make an emergency landing. It had sat next to him when a long-haul return from Amsterdam via Toronto left him so exhausted that his flight to L.A. had to be grounded.

But more precious than the notebook itself was a small, faded slip of paper tucked inside the plastic photo pouch at the back.

It was a currency exchange receipt from Sumitomo Bank—183 U.S. dollars—issued when he left Narita Airport over 40 years ago. And with that memory came a face from the past—Ayako, whom he met in Tokyo.

It was the late summer of 1986 when Taejun visited Tokyo. The trip was for partnership meetings with Japanese companies and a market research tour. As he boarded the plane to Narita Airport, he felt no different than on any other business trip—a window seat and some light paperwork confirming his meeting schedule upon landing. Everything was routine—until a voice gently broke the silence.

"Excuse me, would you like some coffee or tea?"

A voice, soft yet somehow familiar.

When he looked up, a young flight attendant with neatly tied hair stood before him.

Ayako Nishimura.

Her smile was courteous yet warm. Her deep brown eyes conveyed quiet depth, and her crisp uniform highlighted her graceful elegance.

Taejun ordered coffee, and she handed him the cup with practiced ease. Then, after a brief pause, she asked, "Are you traveling for business?"

"Yes. I have a meeting in Tokyo."

She nodded and smiled lightly.

"You have a very nice voice."

That simple comment momentarily made Taejun forget he was on a business trip.

But the plane soon landed, and he couldn't say more to her before heading off toward the airport exit.

~　~　~

The meetings in Tokyo proceeded smoothly. After finishing his official schedule and dinner with partners, Taejun found himself strolling through the streets of Shinjuku.

Then, across the street, he saw a familiar silhouette.

Ayako.

She, too, noticed him, surprised.

"Mr. Kang?"

She remembered his name.

This time, she wasn't in uniform. Her hair was let down softly, and she wore a casual knit sweater and skirt. "I didn't expect to see you again," she said.

She was just about to have a quick dinner at a small ramen shop nearby.

"Have you eaten already?" she asked.

"I have. But ramen... I can always have more."

They entered the cozy ramen shop and shared a warm bowl while talking casually. Ayako opened up about her life as a flight attendant, about traveling the world, and also the loneliness that came with unfamiliar cities.

"Life on the move may look glamorous, but wherever I go, I'm always alone."

At that moment, Taejun realized he, too, shared that same feeling.

Still, they didn't have much time together. She had an overseas flight in two days, and his business schedule remained packed.

"If you have time, I recommend seeing the night view from the Tokyo Tower observatory," she said with a smile.

And with that, they exchanged a reluctant goodbye.

CHAPTER 13

THE BEGINNING OF FIERCE COMPETITION

Taejun was steadily pushing forward with the establishment of Nexora's Korean subsidiary. In the heart of downtown Seoul, surrounded by towering billboards and skyscrapers, he was immersed in busy days, preparing for a new challenge.

However, Seoul was far from a quiet city. In particular, the square in front of City Hall was constantly filled with the shouts of protestors and the blare of loudspeakers. From early morning, crowds would pour in, chanting about various political and social issues, occupying the streets. At times, some aggressive protestors even pushed their way into hotel lobbies. Amid such chaos, Taejun remained unfazed. To maintain focus, he selected the relatively quieter Yeouido district as the office location. As Seoul's financial hub, Yeouido not only offered a stable business environment but also held strategic advantages for Nexora, where foreign exchange transactions were essential.

Taejun decided to lease a building that housed the Yeouido branch of Korea Exchange Bank. As soon as the lease was finalized, preparations for the office launch kicked into high gear. Desks and office supplies were arranged one by one, and network and communication systems were installed, laying the foundation for full-scale operations.

But a bigger challenge than setting up the office was recruiting staff. The entry of a foreign company into the Korean market always drew significant attention. As news of Nexora's Korean subsidiary spread, a flood of job inquiries came in through various channels. Politicians, businesspeople, and even strangers who had never met Taejun tried to pull strings to ask for employment opportunities.

One vice president of a major conglomerate even called Taejun directly, politely yet firmly asking if his daughter could be hired. Taejun declined such requests respectfully, while carefully conducting a thorough hiring process to discover genuinely talented individuals.

Alongside the subsidiary's establishment, Taejun moved swiftly to expand into the Asian market. The Korean market alone was not enough. He planned to visit key markets such as Taiwan, Singapore, and India to strengthen local networks and conduct market research.

In Taiwan, local staff had already scheduled meetings, and Taejun meticulously reviewed the related materials before departure. His schedule in

Taipei was tightly packed, and he had to keep a close eye on the movements of competitors.

While Taejun was preparing for his trip, rival companies were also on high alert. One competitor that had been managing the Korean market remotely from Taipei faced an unexpected crisis. As existing clients gradually switched to Nexora, the company rapidly lost its market share.

Now, survival in the market was no longer just a matter of competition — it was turning into a brutal war. Taejun never let his guard down, determined to win this fight.

CHAPTER 14

BUYING THE FIRST HOME

For immigrants, purchasing a home goes far beyond securing a place to live. It symbolizes stability and achievement, an indication of a life that has taken a significant step forward. When Taejun bought his first home and moved in, he felt an indescribable sense of pride and joy.

Over two years, Taejun saved $30,000 from his company bonuses. He finally used that money as a down payment to purchase his first home. The house he chose was located in an area favored by Asian immigrants, with excellent schools and a reputation for safety, an ideal neighborhood for many East Asian families.

The home he purchased was a cozy single-story house with 1,750 square feet of space. It had three bedrooms, a spacious backyard, and even a small swimming pool. The previous owners, a retired white couple, were planning to buy an RV and travel around the U.S. and Canada for three years, so they put the house on the market. Homes of similar size in that area usually sold for well over $250,000, but the couple wanted to sell quickly, so they listed it for a relatively low price of $230,000. Taejun didn't miss the opportunity and moved forward with the purchase right away.

He secured a 30-year fixed mortgage, and after buying the house, he felt a new sense of emotional stability. Tucked away in a quiet residential area, the house offered a peaceful environment. Since Taejun often traveled for work and was away from home frequently, a safe neighborhood was a must, and this area met that need perfectly.

After buying the house, Taejun adopted Jinny, a dog, along with a rabbit and a hamster. Jinny, a typical energetic Doberman, was well-trained and seemed to enjoy the spacious backyard, which helped ease her stress.

Yujin was also delighted with the new home. She had been giving violin lessons, and now that they had their own place, she could use the living room as a dedicated lesson space. Her students could now visit more comfortably.

The move went smoothly. They brought most of their existing furniture, but also purchased a few new pieces to match the atmosphere of the new home. In the living room, they placed the piano Minseo had wanted, and Taejun set up a study where he could organize his books and documents. A large wardrobe was installed in the bedroom for easier storage, and a small table and chairs were placed in the backyard for relaxing with coffee.

After finally purchasing a home, Taejun truly felt that he had "settled down." It was a moment of realization that all his efforts hadn't been in vain. Despite his busy life, having a place of his own to return to brought him the greatest comfort of all.

CHAPTER 15

A CRITICAL MOMENT – TORONTO - LAX

After completing the week-long International Directors Meeting in Amsterdam, Taejun decided to visit the Toronto office before returning home. Upon arriving in Toronto, he had a conversation with the branch manager and his spouse about the overall industry and discussed future collaboration opportunities.

The reunion led to a long conversation, and as evening approached, the three of them went to a nearby bar for a light meal and some beer. The simple cold sandwiches and a refreshing beer were the perfect way to forget the fatigue, complementing the cold air outside.

However, on Monday morning, the weather in Toronto was bitterly cold. The temperature dropped to -18°C, and the city was frozen. A strong wind brushed against Taejun's face as he headed towards the airport. Upon arriving at the airport and pulling his luggage towards the security checkpoint, something felt wrong. His body felt heavy, and he was drained of energy.

"Could it be from what I ate last night?"

His shoulders bore the weight of a heavy laptop bag, and his other hand held a carry-on suitcase. The airport floor seemed to shake beneath him. Taejun stumbled, struggling to keep his balance, and finally stopped in front of a customs officer.

The officer scanned Taejun from head to toe, then said with a worried look in his eyes:

"You don't look well. Please go to the Nursing Office to get checked."

Following the instructions, Taejun headed towards a small office in the distance. A blue medical symbol was clearly visible above the door. He opened the door and entered, where a nurse in uniform approached and examined his face.

"I'll take your blood pressure."

While the cuff was placed around his arm, Taejun leaned back in the chair. Suddenly, the ceiling seemed to spin.

"I feel dizzy…"

The nurse looked at the blood pressure gauge, and her expression stiffened.

"Your blood pressure is over 180. You're feeling lightheaded, right? You can't board a flight in this condition. You need to go to the emergency room at the hospital right now."

Taejun's mind began to race.

"If I go to the hospital now, the company will find out. If health problems interfere with my work, I might face penalties..."

Fear rushed through him. But there was something more worrying.

"Yujin has to come. What about David? He's only three years old... Can Yujin come here while leaving the kids behind?"

His mind was filled with complicated thoughts. Taejun spoke decisively.

"No, I need to board the plane."

The nurse frowned and tried to convince him, but Taejun stood firm.

After 30 minutes of back-and-forth, the nurse sighed and said:

"Alright. But there's one option. Once you're on the plane, after about 30 minutes, tell the flight attendants you're having chest pains. It'll be hard to land immediately after the plane has gained altitude, but you might make it to LA."

The nurse prescribed temporary blood pressure medication. Taejun slowly stood up, smiled in response, and walked toward the gate.

His head was spinning, but the fear of letting the company find out was stronger than anything else.

~ ~ ~

The flight Taejun was on was a long-haul international flight from Toronto to LA, then on to Hawaii and Sydney, Australia. The plane was full.

After takeoff, Taejun waited for 30 minutes as instructed by the nurse. He struggled to stay awake, pinching his thighs and moving his legs to fight off sleep.

Finally, after the time passed, he called a flight attendant who was passing by.

"My chest hurts…"

He grimaced in pain, his face contorted. The flight attendant's face instantly turned pale.

"Please wait a moment."

The flight attendant quickly went to call the purser. An announcement came over the intercom:

"Is there a doctor on board? One of our passengers is experiencing a health emergency."

The passengers around him murmured and stared at Taejun. Some looked on with a mix of curiosity and concern, while others stood, watching the situation unfold.

Fortunately, there was a doctor on board. The purser immediately called for the doctor, and the doctor presented his license for identity verification.

The captain sent it to ground control for confirmation. A few minutes later, the verification was complete, and the doctor began his examination.

Taejun's shirt was removed, and the blood pressure cuff was placed on his arm. The purser was in close contact with the captain, discussing the possibility of an emergency landing.

"His blood pressure is too high. We need to land immediately."

The doctor was firm, but Taejun shook his head.

"Let's go a little further. If it gets worse, then we'll decide."

The captain stayed in contact with ground control, carefully monitoring the situation. All the passengers' eyes were on Taejun, but in his mind, only David's face was in focus.

~ ~ ~

After a 6-hour flight, they arrived at LAX. An announcement came on the intercom:

"All passengers are asked to remain seated. A medical team is boarding."

Outside the window, several ambulances and fire trucks were parked with their sirens blaring.

While all the passengers were waiting, strong paramedics entered the cabin and lifted Taejun onto a stretcher. He was quickly transported to the hospital via a back entrance at the airport.

At 4 a.m., Taejun was discharged after receiving emergency treatment. He took a taxi home.

When he arrived, Yujin opened the door with a shocked expression.

"What happened? Why didn't you say anything?"

Taejun weakly smiled.

Looking at David and Minseo, who were deeply asleep in the living room, Taejun felt a sense of relief.

"I'm home."

CHAPTER 16

AUTUMN 1989, PARIS

The sunset seeped through the window. Taejun sat at his study desk and took out an old leather notebook. His fingers gently stroked the worn-out cover.

"It might be time… to finally record the path I've walked."

After more than forty years in the wilderness, fighting countless winds, Taejun decided to write an autobiography, a reflection of his life. He opened his laptop and typed like he was striking the keys of a typewriter. The first sentence appeared on the screen:

"In 1982, I stepped onto this land with nothing but $183 in my pocket."

And suddenly, memories came rushing in like waves.

He remembered landing at Honolulu Airport, holding Minseo's hand tightly during immigration inspection, and how Yujin worked at a laundromat to make ends meet…

His hand touched the back pouch of the notebook. Old business cards were still tucked inside. His eyes stopped on one of them.

Autumn 1989, Paris

When the plane landed at Charles de Gaulle Airport in Paris, Taejun took a deep breath. The heavy air of the airport seemed to carry a subtle scent of bitter wine. Riding a taxi into the city center, he gazed out at the classic buildings and the Seine slicing through the city.

"This city is different."

No scorching sun of Los Angeles, no fast-paced rhythm of Seoul. Even amidst a tight business schedule, Taejun felt that this trip might offer him a moment to reflect, wrapped in unfamiliar air.

He unpacked at the Concorde Hotel, near the beginning of the Champs-Élysées.

The meeting room at French partner Moreau & Co. had a modern flair. Through the window, the Eiffel Tower loomed in the distance, and the afternoon sun poured softly through the large glass panes.

"Welcome, Mr. Kang."

A woman's voice pronounced his Korean name with a graceful accent. Taejun slowly turned his head.

Chadwick Moreau.

She was the international director and lead negotiator for Moreau & Co. With her dark brown hair tied up and dressed in a beige suit, Chadwick exuded a natural sophistication. Her eyes mirrored the deep blue of the Seine, and behind thin gold-rimmed glasses, she radiated intelligence.

"We've been expecting you, Mr. Kang."

Her smile was formal, yet Taejun sensed a subtle curiosity beneath it.

Taejun and Chadwick proceeded with their contract negotiations, discussing the French market and Korean distribution networks. As the talks progressed, Chadwick found herself drawn to Taejun's business philosophy and daring spirit. Once the deal was successfully wrapped up, she extended an invitation for dinner.

"If you're in Paris, you must enjoy some good wine."

That evening, Taejun and Chadwick headed to a small bar along the Seine. The name of the bar was *Le Rêve Bleu*—"The Blue Dream."

Unlike Tokyo or Seoul, Parisian nights weren't fast-paced, nor as glamorous as New York. In the dim candlelight of the bar, soft jazz played in the background. Chadwick ordered a bottle of 1982 Château Margaux.

"This wine needs six years before it truly reveals its flavor," she said, tilting her glass.

"I'm used to waiting," Taejun replied, raising his.

Over wine, Taejun shared stories of his struggles in Korea and the tough life of an immigrant in America.

Chadwick opened up as well. She explained how she settled in Paris alone after a divorce, and commented on the challenges of surviving in the male-dominated business world.

Back in his hotel room, he took off his shirt and stared into the mirror.

His face bore the fatigue—and a trace of loneliness.

Have I gone too deep into the world of business…?

He fell onto the bed and sank into thought.

CHAPTER 17

MOSCOW, MEMORIES OF RED SQUARE

Taejun stared at the television news, lost in deep thought. The news was filled with daily reports of the war in Ukraine—cities ablaze, tanks rolling through the streets, violent clashes unfolding. As he watched the screen, memories from long ago surfaced naturally in his mind.

August 1991, Moscow.

He had been there at the very moment the Soviet Union was collapsing.

Sunday night, August 18, 1991

It had been over nine hours since Korean Air flight KE5923 departed from Gimpo Airport. Taejun looked out at the dark sky beyond the plane's window while skimming through documents. He was on a business trip to attend an international conference in Moscow.

It had been a year since he acquired U.S. citizenship. Holding an American passport made him feel more secure, which helped him decide to go on this trip. Yet, deep down, an inexplicable unease lingered. He had visited Beijing several times before, but Moscow felt different. It was the capital of the Soviet Union, a strictly communist nation, and tension crept over him as he entered that unfamiliar place.

When the plane landed at Moscow International Airport, Taejun entered the immigration hall and immediately noticed the immigration officers in military uniforms. Each had two large stars on both shoulders. Were they soldiers or officials? The power of the military was clearly embedded in the atmosphere, and cold sweat ran down Taejun's back.

After completing immigration procedures, he exchanged currency at the airport and caught a taxi to the Cosmos Hotel. It was late at night, and uniformed guards were lined up at the hotel entrance. He couldn't tell whether they were military or civilian. Taejun quickly checked in and entered his room. After unpacking and taking a brief shower, he studied a map in preparation for the next day's meeting.

~ ~ ~

The next morning, the alarm rang. Taejun put on a suit and had a simple breakfast in the hotel restaurant. As he sipped his coffee, he thought about the day's conference. The meeting at the

International Convention Center was scheduled to begin at 10 a.m.

Around 9 a.m., he called a taxi from the hotel and headed for the convention center. But as soon as he arrived, he couldn't believe his eyes.

"Conference is cancelled."

A large sign hung at the main entrance of the center.

"What's going on?"

Confused, Taejun asked a few people nearby. The response was shocking.

"There's been a coup!"

A coup?

Taejun felt momentarily stunned.

On the early morning of Monday, August 19, 1991, conservative factions within the Soviet military had staged a coup to oust President Mikhail

Gorbachev. The streets were nearly empty. The entire city seemed to be holding its breath.

Taejun had to return to his hotel, but there wasn't a taxi in sight. Rain was pouring down, and he stood alone in the middle of the road in his suit.

Then he noticed a large bus parked in front of the convention center. Without hesitation, he boarded the bus.

"Cosmos Hotel! Cosmos Hotel!"

He shouted to the driver, but the driver simply stared at him. Taejun quickly pulled a $100 bill from his wallet and placed it in the driver's hand.

At that moment, the driver's expression changed.

The engine started.

Later, Taejun would learn that at the time, $100 was equivalent to a Russian professor's annual salary—a fortune.

He held onto the rail and remained standing. The bus drove through the empty streets for about an hour.

~   ~   ~

Back at the hotel, Taejun immediately turned on CNN.

Red Square filled the screen.

Tanks lined the roads, and soldiers stood expressionless in formation. Russian citizens were gathering in the square, and chants erupted in various places. Foreign guests in the hotel lobby gathered in front of the TV, watching the urgent news unfold.

Taejun thought about how worried his family in America must be. But there was no way to contact them directly from the hotel. He decided to go to the U.S. Embassy himself. The next morning, he stepped out into the rainy streets. The walk from the

Cosmos Hotel to the embassy took about two hours. Protesters and soldiers mingled in the streets.

At the embassy, security was tight. U.S. Marines asked Taejun to remove his belt and shoes for screening. For a moment, he wondered if it was racial profiling, but he complied.

After quickly registering his identity, he walked back to the hotel through the rain.

~ ~ ~

Due to the coup, Korean Air was unlikely to arrive on schedule. Taejun began urgently looking for other flights.

Fortunately, he managed to get a Moscow–Zurich ticket with Swissair. However, the price was three times the usual—$850. There was no time to hesitate. He had to leave, no matter what.

Wednesday afternoon, August 21

While riding a taxi to the airport, he saw numerous tanks withdrawing on the opposite side of the road.

The driver said,

"The coup is over."

Taejun was startled.

"It's over?"

"Yes, it failed."

From the radio, Boris Yeltsin's voice echoed. He had climbed onto a tank and was denouncing the coup before the people.

In the end, the coup failed after just two days. But it wasn't merely a failure.

It was the collapse of the Soviet Union.

~ ~ ~

Upon arriving at the airport, Taejun stood in a long line for departure inspection.

When it was his turn, he handed his passport to the soldier at the counter. The soldier stared at him so intensely that it felt piercing.

For a brief moment, Taejun couldn't breathe.

What if they don't let me leave? That fleeting instant was filled with dread.

Then, with a loud "thud," the exit stamp was placed in his passport, and it was handed back.

That night, Taejun landed at Zurich Airport.

The air felt different. He took a deep breath. As soon as he checked into his hotel, he called home in the U.S.

Yujin and the family had been extremely worried.

It was summer break, and Yujin had taken the children on a trip to the Grand Canyon. She had heard about the Moscow coup through friends. With their help, she contacted the U.S. State Department and confirmed Taejun's whereabouts and safety.

His company had also begun making contingency plans to ensure their employees' safety.

After spending a day in Zurich, Taejun went on to Paris, where he rested for three days. The few days in Moscow felt like a dream. He had witnessed history firsthand—and survived.

CHAPTER 18

RISING AGAIN AMID THE STORM

After establishing Nexora's Korea branch, Taejun had been relentlessly focused on expanding into the Asian market. From Taipei and Singapore to New Delhi, his reach was growing wider. However, internal discord within the company was also intensifying.

A year earlier, Victoria, the international division president at headquarters, had created a new position titled "Vice President of Asia-Pacific Operations." It was a role that covered as far as Australia and New Zealand, and Jonathan—a former executive from the computer hardware industry—was brought in to fill it. Based in Tokyo, Japan, he had high mobility. He lived with his Japanese wife and two daughters, and amusingly claimed to have learned Korean at a place called "Kirao Kkejujeom."

From the beginning, Taejun felt uneasy around Jonathan. Jonathan was not pleased about Taejun's close relationship with Patterson, the president at headquarters. Victoria, too, was uncomfortable with Taejun's personal rapport with Patterson. The creation of Jonathan's new role had been a strategic move to keep Taejun in check.

Taejun couldn't shake the feeling that Jonathan was actively trying to undermine him to gain influence at headquarters. The tension worsened when Jonathan requested that a woman he knew be hired as a full-time employee at the Seoul branch. Taejun refused.

After that, whenever Taejun returned to his home in LA from business trips to Korea, Jonathan would drop by the Seoul office to build rapport with the employees, as if he were trying to fill Taejun's absence.

One day, Jonathan unexpectedly showed up in Seoul and asked to meet Taejun. They met in a basement café.

"Taejun, let's work together," Jonathan said.

Taejun tensed. He wasn't sure what Jonathan truly meant.

There was a subtle hint of pressure in Jonathan's voice.

This wasn't just a proposal for cooperation. Jonathan was trying to draw him in—or it could be a trap.

Jonathan stopped stirring his coffee and stared intently at Taejun.

"You know as well as I do—we could draw a bigger picture if we join forces."

Taejun calmly held his gaze.

"I have to stick to my principles."

Jonathan's face hardened.

After more than four hours of conversation, Taejun was increasingly convinced. It was time to go down a different path.

And so, he left the company due to the ongoing conflict with Jonathan.

Taejun decided to reduce his overseas travel and focus on finding new opportunities within the U.S.

Around that time, a cosmetics company in Seoul, Maria Cosmetics, offered him exclusive U.S. distribution rights.

"Cosmetics? That's a field I know nothing about…"

Still, he was experienced in trade, and there was no reason to shy away from a new challenge.

Taejun leased a warehouse in LA and ordered a container of products. He began recruiting regional distributors, ran newspaper ads, and contacted Korean markets to place the products on their shelves.

The container arrived, the products were stocked, and sales were just beginning.

April 29, 1992.

The LA riots broke out.

Angered by the Rodney King verdict, mobs attacked shops and set buildings ablaze indiscriminately.

Taejun was speechless as he watched the TV screen.

The broadcast showed Korean shopkeepers on rooftops, armed and defending their stores.

"No…"

His own warehouse was engulfed in flames.

All the cosmetics in the container, the equipment—everything was destroyed.

He hadn't even gotten insurance yet, so there was no hope for compensation.

Yujin cried.

"But you weren't hurt. That means you can start over."

Taejun clenched his fist.

"I will rise again…"

A few weeks later, Taejun thought of a Saudi Arabian trader he had worked with in the past.

To his surprise, the trader told him that he was planning to open a department store in Moscow and was currently looking for Korean cosmetics.

"I'm saved!"

The Saudi trader opened an L/C (letter of credit) at Taejun's U.S. bank, and Taejun, in turn, issued a credit line in Korea. This allowed Maria Cosmetics to ship directly to Moscow—a triangular trade structure.

Korean cosmetics being sold in a Moscow department store!

The Saudi buyer also hinted at future expansions into apparel, fashion, and food.

Taejun felt as though the wounds from the riot were slowly beginning to heal.

But hope was short-lived.

Just as everything was coming together, one morning Taejun arrived at the office to find a fax from Maria Cosmetics.

"There is a risk that the temperature in Moscow may drop below -15°C in January, which could result in the products freezing. Shipment will be postponed."

If the products froze and shattered, the Saudi buyer would certainly file a claim. So Maria Cosmetics refused to ship them at all.

Taejun tried to explain the situation to the buyer and suggested delaying the shipment until March.

But the Saudi side strongly objected.

"How can we open a department store without merchandise?" they argued.

"If you delay until March, we will cancel the contract!"

Taejun turned pale.

This had been his last chance to revive his business…

But he had no other choice.

"The cosmetics business is over."

The order was canceled. Everything dissolved into nothing.

He calmly accepted reality.

"I have to rise again."

Back to square one.

Time passed, and Taejun thought of a British multinational company called Innoforge.

They had once tried to recruit him when he was with Nexora.

He reached out to Taylor, the president of their North American division.

"It's time for me to return."

Taylor contacted Collins, the Vice President of International Operations at their London headquarters.

Three weeks later, Taejun visited the North American headquarters in Seattle and negotiated salary, contract terms, and title with VP Collins. They agreed to appoint him as Director of Asia and to establish Asia headquarters in both LA and Seoul.

"I'm returning to the corporate world."

He took a deep breath.

It was a new opportunity—something he hadn't even dared to dream of in a while.

Taejun's life was once again facing a bold new challenge.

CHAPTER 19

THE ENGINE CAUGHT FIRE

After returning to the British multinational company *Innoforge* as Director of Asian Operations, Taejun had been building a passionate career in peace. But once again, an unstoppable storm was rolling toward him.

Starting in the second half of 1997, foreign exchange issues began to surface in Korea.

By November, the currency crisis erupted, and society fell into chaos. The dollar, which used to be worth 800–900 won, soared to 1,700 won by year-end and reached 1,965 won in early January. Banks and companies were unable to make dollar payments overseas. Taejun's clients had budgeted at around 900 won per dollar, but now they needed almost double the amount in Korean won.

At the start of the year, foreign capital withdrew rapidly, the won plummeted in value, and companies began to fall into bankruptcy one after another. On November 21, the Korean government finally requested a bailout from the IMF. This wasn't just a financial crisis — it was a national upheaval.

Phones on Taejun's desk rang relentlessly.

"What the hell is going on?"

The voice from the London HQ's finance team was sharp and tense.

Taejun quickly skimmed through the report he received from the accounting manager.

"There are already several million dollars in unpaid balances."

The paper in his hand became damp with sweat.

What am I supposed to do now?

Neither his Korean clients nor the London headquarters had a solution.

He tried to explain the Korean situation to HQ as sincerely as he could, but their distrust toward Korea—and Taejun—only grew stronger.

The financial damage was too severe.

As the year passed, sales in Korea became impossible to predict, eventually dropping to less than half. Taejun's position within headquarters also weakened. Although the crisis had been beyond his control, the Korean branch's performance was in the red, and the expense budget was being cut.

Taejun could feel it.

I might have to pack my bags again…

Time passed amidst chaos, and the market showed no signs of recovery. Then came the U.S. financial crisis—another blow.

To submit a comprehensive report to the London Group headquarters, Taejun left LA and headed for London via New York. In New York, he planned to meet with his former boss Patterson, chairman of Omnizon, to discuss future collaboration. Patterson was engrossed in building an e-commerce platform and planning to take the company public on NASDAQ, aiming to raise over $500 million through an IPO.

He also met with Brian, the former European regional head from the 1980s and 1990s, now an international executive—an old friend and colleague. They shared a warm lunch and conversation.

~ ~ ~

February 20, 1999, 7:00 PM – Flight to London

It was a quiet Saturday evening. Traffic to the airport was light, and the terminal wasn't crowded.

After a light dinner in the lounge, Taejun boarded the flight. His seat was at the far rear on the right, but luckily, it was an aisle seat. He looked out the window to see the massive engine attached to the wing and the ground crew bustling around.

This flight would go from New York to London, then to Riyadh, and finally to Hong Kong—a long-haul, fully booked flight.

Departing at 7 PM, he planned to arrive at Heathrow on Sunday morning, take the airport bus, and head into the city.

The woman sitting next to him wore a strong perfume, making it hard to breathe. He couldn't turn toward the window, so he tilted his head left toward the aisle to catch his breath, quietly covering his nose so she wouldn't notice. It was suffocating.

With the cabin full, there was no way to change seats.

How am I supposed to endure seven hours like this?

A flight announcement came over the speakers.

"Ladies and gentlemen, thank you for your patience. We are now ready for departure."

The aircraft slowly moved away from the gate and began heading to the runway.

Once there, the crew asked passengers to fasten their seatbelts once again. The plane gradually picked up speed. As it accelerated down the runway and lifted into the sky, Taejun's body leaned back in his seat.

He turned his head slightly to the right, peeking through the window at the terminal disappearing below. Five or six minutes had passed. The aircraft continued to ascend steeply, reaching cruising altitude.

Then—suddenly—a spark burst, illuminating the night sky. Right before his eyes, Taejun saw the right engine flare up like lightning and then erupt in flames.

Oh my god… The engine's on fire!

A warning alarm blared in the cabin.

"Ladies and gentlemen, we are experiencing a technical issue. Please prepare for an emergency landing."

The cabin lights were turned off.

Darkness.

The cabin filled with gasps, murmurs, and stifled cries.

The captain shut down the right engine.

Moments later, the fire was extinguished.

A heavy silence fell over the cabin.

Taejun gripped the armrest tightly and closed his eyes.

Oxygen masks dropped. Flight attendants shouted emergency instructions.

The pilot circled over the ocean near New York for about an hour, dumping fuel—because excess fuel poses a greater risk of fire during an emergency landing.

The aircraft turned back toward the airport.

After circling several times, it secured a runway at the far end. Passengers were instructed to brace themselves—hands forward, heads down, against the seat in front.

Is this the end?

A flood of memories surged through Taejun's mind.

Seventeen years ago, he had exchanged $183 at Narita Airport and boarded a flight to America.

He was terrified then, too.

Can I really survive in a new country?

His heart had pounded like this before, when everything was uncertain.

From the air, he could see flashing red lights from dozens of fire trucks and ambulances surrounding the runway.

Taejun held his breath, burying his head, eyes closed tight.

Faces of Yujin, Minseo, and David flashed before him.

The aircraft barely managed a successful emergency landing.

What is life?

Why is it so perilous?

Back at the gate, passengers were divided into two groups: those too afraid to continue, and those willing to board another plane to London.

Taejun hesitated, clenching and unclenching his hands repeatedly.

Then, he dialed Yujin's number.

"Hello?"

"Taejun! Are you okay? I just saw the news. The plane… It was really serious, wasn't it?"

Her voice trembled. He could feel her panic through the line.

Taejun closed his eyes briefly. More than the moment his life was in danger, this—hearing his family's fear—was more suffocating.

"I'm okay. But… I have to go to London."

"What? After all that, you're getting on another flight?"

Her voice rose with alarm.

"Taejun, your life is more important than your job! Can't you cancel this trip?"

He exhaled deeply. If he skipped the business trip now, with the Korean branch collapsing, he'd completely lose headquarters' trust. His position in London was already on thin ice. If he missed this chance, there would be no way back.

"Yujin, I know. But if I back out now, they'll stop believing in me. I have to be there myself—to defend the Korean market."

Yujin couldn't speak for a moment, choked with emotion.

"…Fine. Just promise me one thing. Come back safe."

Taejun nodded silently.

~ ~ ~

At the re-boarding counter, a member of the airline staff said, "Sir, your seat has been upgraded to business class."

Taejun raised his brows in surprise, then smiled faintly.

Maybe this is a small gift from the heavens.

As he sat in business class and looked out the window, he realized—this time, he didn't have to hold his breath.

The seat next to him was empty.

October 31 – The Day of the Merger

On the last day of October, Taejun arrived at the office earlier than usual. But from early morning, a strange rumor was already circulating among employees.

"Our company's being merged!"

His mind went blank for a moment.

As soon as he opened his email, the official announcement from headquarters appeared on the screen.

"Technoir Group and Innoforge have decided on a strategic merger."

Taejun took a sip of coffee.

Now what will become of me…?

It was, in effect, a takeover. The French company Technoir was absorbing the British firm Innoforge.

Taejun scheduled an interview in early December with Greg, the Asia-Pacific Vice President of Technoir Group, to discuss the future of his position.

~ ~ ~

Seoul, Namsan Hilton Hotel Café

Outside the window, the Seoul cityscape was blurred with haze.

Taejun sat at a table, slowly turning his coffee cup while taking a deep breath.

The door opened. A tall man with cold eyes entered. It was Greg.

With calculated movements, he took a seat and scanned Taejun briefly.

"Nice to meet you."

Taejun extended his hand, but Greg only gave a light handshake and got straight to the point.

"Mr. Kang, as the current Korea Country Manager, I'd like to hear your plans moving forward."

There was no room for pleasantries. His tone was direct, even blunt.

Taejun tried to maintain a calm smile, though his fingers tensed slightly.

This isn't an interview. It's a trial.

He straightened his posture and spoke with composure.

"With the merger between Technoir Group and Innoforge, I believe new opportunities have opened up.

In particular, the Korean market can serve as a strategic hub for all of Asia—"

"Are you sure?"

Greg interrupted. He dropped a set of papers onto the table.

"If the Korean market is so important, then why are this year's numbers a disaster?"

Taejun's heart sank. The papers detailed the Korean branch's revenue and expense reports line by line.

"After the currency crisis, the market contracted rapidly, and the recovery has been slower than expected. But—"

"But?"

Greg picked up his coffee cup, wearing a faint sneer.

"In my view, it's not about 'but.' It's about results. Is there a clear reason to keep the Korean branch running?"

Taejun refused to retreat. He drew a breath and replied with firm resolve.

"Mr. Greg, if Technoir Group wants to lead the Asian market, the Korean branch is essential.

Yes, we're in a crisis, but if we treat this merger as an opportunity, we can restructure and—"

"Restructure?"

Greg chuckled.

"Mr. Kang, let's be honest. Are you prepared to leave this company?"

Silence fell between them.

Taejun held Greg's gaze. In his eyes, the decision had already been made.

This is no longer a seat I can protect.

But he didn't waver.

"Whatever direction the company chooses, I will give my best until the end."

Greg gave a meaningful nod.

"Very well. You'll be hearing from us soon."

Then he stood and walked away without a shred of hesitation.

Taejun let out a long breath.

So… what happens to me now?

~ ~ ~

December 30, 10:00 AM – The Final Call

The Seoul branch office was unusually quiet. Was it the year-end lull? Or an ominous sign?

The phone on his desk rang.

Caller ID: "Bennett, HR Director."

Taejun stared at the phone for a moment, then slowly picked up the receiver.

"Hello, Bennett speaking. Is this a good time, Mr. Kang?"

The voice was crisp, with a classic British accent—cool and composed.

"Yes, Bennett. I assume this is about the integration process?"

Taejun tried to maintain a steady tone.

"Indeed. I'll get straight to the point. The executive team has completed its final review of the Korea office structure. As you know, following the Technoir–Innoforge merger, some organizational adjustments were inevitable."

Taejun already knew the answer, but he waited to hear it in full.

"And?"

"We regret to inform you that your position as Korea Country Manager will not be retained moving forward."

His mind went blank.

"…I see."

"We appreciate your years of service, and we'll provide a severance package in accordance with global policy. The official notice will be sent via email within the hour. Your transition period will last until the end of next month."

They weren't even giving him time to clean out his desk.

"Understood. May I ask—was this decision solely based on cost-cutting?"

There was a short silence.

"Partially, yes. But ultimately, leadership decided that we don't need two senior managers in Korea. Mr. Greg will oversee all regional operations moving forward."

Greg... so that's how it ends. Taejun drew in a breath and said, "Thank you for your transparency, Bennett."

"I understand this is difficult, Mr. Kang. But as you always say—when one door closes, another opens."

Taejun smiled faintly. He hadn't expected Bennett to quote his own motto back to him.

"Yes. I suppose you're right."

He hung up and rose from his chair, walking slowly toward the window.

Outside, the air was sharp with winter's chill. Six years of his life—all ending here. But… this wasn't the end.

He drew in a deep breath and whispered to himself, "There's nothing to fear. I'll start again."

And a small smile appeared on his lips.

CHAPTER 20

THE BUBBLE

Taejun watched the news, catching a report on the stock market on CNBC. Memories from over twenty years ago—of the dot-com bubble—resurfaced, and he fell into deep thought.

Though he had lived through countless events, the experience and loss from that time still left a deep scar. The golden era of his life, followed by another fall.

Having left the British company, Taejun was absorbed in planning how to navigate the 2000s.

Then, through Brian in New York, he received contact from Chairman Patterson of Ominizon. Just as he was regaining his footing with the new year, Taejun wondered if this was a new opportunity. They had met during a trip to New York a year prior, and Chairman Patterson was aware that Taejun had stepped down following a corporate merger.

Taejun booked a flight and flew straight to New York.

Chairman Patterson had secured over $500 million through the IPO of a newly listed e-commerce platform and was aggressively acquiring companies to build a global system.

Brian, now the international president overseeing Europe, Asia, North and South America, was reorganizing the structure and consolidating departments. Taejun had a close relationship with Brian dating back to the '80s and '90s, when Taejun led the Asia division and Brian was president of Europe.

Brian made him an offer: To take charge of Asia, including Korea, and lead the Korean local corporation. He also asked Taejun's opinion on acquiring a Korean company as a local base. The salary and bonus package offered was on a whole different scale compared to his previous job. Taejun realized again how important personal relationships are—even in the U.S.

On his way back to LA, Taejun felt like he's dreaming. After leaving the company due to the merger between Innoforge and Technoir, a new world is opening up for him.

He sensed a hope that he can rise to the top again.

Establishing a legal entity in Seoul and searching for a Korean company to acquire, Taejun proceeded with due diligence through a law firm. He feels alive again. He set up a place to stay in Yeouido and spends weekends at the Lotte Hotel.

Taejun's life was once again full of vitality. Unexpected executive stock options brought him joy. The company's shares on NASDAQ were trading at $36, and he was granted shares at $5.31.

He took his employees out for group movie nights and holds negotiations for acquiring a local company at 'Ojinam,' a high-end restaurant known to have hosted former presidents. He planed to purchase more company stock and hold it long-term.

Taejun returned temporarily to attend his daughter Minseo's college graduation on Korean Air flight KE017. The family gathered to celebrate at the Wilshire Grand Hotel ballroom. While discussing Minseo's future, Taejun made a suggestion.

"Minseo, go to Paris. How about getting your MBA there?"

Minseo had studied French since high school and had visited Paris a couple of times.

Taejun recalled a past conversation with Chairman Patterson. He had received a call from Betty, the chairman's secretary. Patterson had a seminar at Irvine Memorial Hospital and asked if Taejun could pick him up from John Wayne Airport and drive him to the hospital. Taejun gladly accepted.

Taejun's car was small, so he felt a bit awkward chauffeuring the chairman, but he had no choice.

On the way to the hospital, as silence fell, Taejun asked a question to break the awkwardness:

"Dr. Patterson, what do you think of the American Dream? What's your definition?"

Patterson, who held a PhD in philosophy from Harvard, was referred to as "Dr. Patterson" by his employees.

He answered: "Education."

It was a surprisingly concise answer. For nearly twenty years after that, Taejun held the belief that providing a good education for one's children was the true path to achieving the American Dream.

He decided to send Minseo to Paris for graduate studies. The company continued to grow as new funding flows in.

One early autumn Tuesday evening, Taejun returned to his lodging after a client meeting in Daejeon, having taken the Saemaeul train. It's a little past 8 p.m. As he removed his suit jacket and turns on the TV, CNN was showing the New York skyline with smoke rising from the World Trade Center.

"What is this?" He stopped mid-motion and walked toward the TV. Soon, a plane flew into the frame and crashed into the building.

"Ah!" Taejun cried out. He could not sleep that night, watching the chaos unfold in New York.

Grief and outrage brought him to tears.

Evil truly exists. People with minds beyond comprehension attack innocent lives.

He lacked the energy to go to work, informed the company that he would be taking the day off, and stayed in bed all day. How could such a thing happen? His secretary, Yang, visited him after work to express her concern.

An email arrived from headquarters: the global strategy division was calling for a meeting of all overseas branch managers.

Although these meetings were routine, recent news of countless internet companies going bankrupt had left the industry unsettled, and the meeting's atmosphere was tense. The company stock had reached an all-time high of $86, and Taejun had recently been granted additional stock options at $30-something.

But two months after returning to Seoul, the stock began to decline. As other internet companies collapsed, funding dried up. Of the ten or so companies they had merged with, many were now failing due to a lack of capital.

Taejun felt anxious. Although the Korean subsidiary still had enough cash, the parent company's worsening financial situation was dragging the stock price down to the $3 range. All of this unfolded in just a few weeks. When the stock hit $1, an acquisition proposal came in, and the CFO sent an email stating that negotiations had begun.

Taejun realized that he might have to return to square one. If the company went bankrupt, the stock options would become worthless. Even more concerning was the growing unrest among his staff.

Taejun sent an email to all employees informing them of the situation. Some threatened to report him to the labor ministry. This all happened within just a month or two.

Taejun contacted a law firm to handle layoffs and respond to legal threats. Now he was tasked with handing over operations to the acquiring firm. That company also had a branch in Korea, and Taejun had to work with its manager. The man behaved like a conquering general.

Even in despair, Taejun started thinking about survival again—about starting something new. His mind felt heavy. The handover continued for over a year. But no one in this world knew what tomorrow holds.

The American parent company that had acquired Taejun's company had, over time, bought more than thirty tech firms, but none delivered results. Burdened with losses, the company finally files for bankruptcy.

What an irony.

Taejun was once again the representative of a hollow shell—the Korean subsidiary. He spent five years at this second venture with Chairman Patterson's Internet E-commerce Platform company, and now, once again, he found himself alone.

Taejun boarded Korean Air flight KE011, a nighttime departure, and began his journey home. Would he be able to return to Seoul? Would he ever set foot in Asia again?

The soaring glory and the crash of the past five years! However, the sunset was beautiful. Surely, another world will open.

CHAPTER 21

PYEONGCHANG-DONG

Whenever Taejun visited New York, he always stayed at the Sheraton Center New York near 7th Avenue and Times Square. He enjoyed musicals nearby and occasionally took walks to Central Park. The first time he came to the U.S. on a business trip for the Toy Fair, he stayed at that same hotel.

Late autumn, 2003, in New York.

One afternoon, as Central Park's leaves turned crimson, Taejun, having wrapped up his exhibition schedule, was walking around the fair booths. It was a major event with many Korean internet companies participating.

That's when he noticed a Korean woman in the distance, fluently speaking English with a foreign buyer. She had a stylish outfit, neat hair, and a natural smile.

As he passed by without much thought, their eyes met. It was Jiyeon.

"Oh? Aren't you… Mr. Kang Taejun?"

A familiar face. Taejun soon recalled her. A few years ago, they had briefly met at a gathering in Seoul. Back then, she was temporarily working as an interpreter for a construction materials company at a trade fair. Her actual job was a flight attendant for an American airline.

"Jiyeon… It's been a while."

She responded with a bright smile.

"Are you here on a business trip too?"

"Yes. And you?"

"I work for a trading company now. I help introduce Korean brands to overseas markets."

After a brief conversation at the fair, they agreed to have coffee that evening. That night, the two walked through Central Park, talking.

"You quit being a flight attendant?"

"Yes… for several reasons."

Jiyeon hesitated for a moment and let out a light sigh.

"I heard you live in New York?"

"No, I'm based in Seoul. Just here on a short trip." Brushing her hair back in the autumn breeze, Jiyeon added, "To be honest… I don't have good memories of New York."

Her gaze drifted off into the distance.

"Why is that?" Taejun asked gently, but she shook her head slightly.

"If I told you… It would be a very long story."

That evening, Taejun didn't ask further. She smiled quietly, but behind that smile, he sensed a deep wound.

~ ~ ~

A few months later, they met again in Seoul. It was a small café in a quiet alley in Pyeongchang-dong. On a snowy winter night, Jiyeon quietly began to speak.

"Mr. Kang, I'll tell you now why I came to hate New York."

Taking a sip of tea, she began her story calmly.

"I quit flying and got married. He was a Korean-American living in New York. A taekwondo instructor. We met by chance on a flight. He was gentle and kind. I thought we'd be happy living in New York together after marriage. "At the time, life in Korea was really hard for me. I had family issues…"

Jiyeon gave a bitter smile as she continued. "But something felt wrong from the first night of our honeymoon. He avoided me. He said he was tired. Even after days, he wouldn't come near me. In the end, I found out. He had a serious back injury and couldn't have a normal married life."

Taejun listened silently.

"He didn't marry me out of love. He needed someone to take care of his mother back in Daejeon. Even after we married, he stayed in New York, while I waited for the invitation letter to join him. I lived in Daejeon, caring for his mother. We had no honeymoon, no home of our own. I wasn't a wife. I was a caregiver. I lived like that for two years."

Finishing the last sip of her tea, Jiyeon spoke quietly. "In the end, I filed for divorce. Two years later, the marriage was annulled."

Jiyeon's father was a pastor. Her mother had passed away from illness, and her stepmother was cold and harsh. She grew up under constant mistreatment and applied to an American airline to escape her home. With excellent English and a polished appearance, she was hired immediately and mainly flew the New York route.

Looking out the window, Jiyeon said softly,

"That's when I first learned that people can use other people."

Taejun looked at her, but maintained his silence.

"Still… I'm okay now," she said. "The scars have all faded."

But he noticed her fingertips trembling ever so slightly. He spoke gently. "You're a strong person, Jiyeon."

She smiled and replied,

"I'm just pretending to be strong."

That night, Taejun walked her home. A snowy hill in Pyeongchang-dong. As she got out of the car, she said, "Would you like to come in for a cup of coffee? Sometimes, just having someone to listen can be comforting."

The living room was modest but warm.

As Jiyeon hung up her coat, Taejun saw tears welling up in her eyes.

Looking at her quietly, he said, "Whenever you feel like talking, don't hesitate to call me."

She looked up at the snowy night sky outside the window and smiled gently.

"This afternoon, I received the court's final ruling. I'm coming from there now."

At that moment, Taejun was at a loss for words.

CHAPTER 22

A New World

In a corner of Taejun's study sits a retired electric rice cooker, tucked away on a bookshelf. It's a one-person rice cooker that he would always take with him on his business trips. It's been nearly 50 years since the first business trip.

After finishing his corporate career and returning to the U.S., Taejun planned to settle down and raise his children, putting an end to his days of constant travel. He felt it was time to start and grow his own small business. With some financial cushion still available, he considered acquiring a small company. With an SBA loan and a bit of working capital, he thought he could buy a small retail business and run it locally.

However, Taejun had no experience running a retail shop, which made it daunting. Instead, he decided to leverage his corporate background and management expertise by focusing on the service sector. He began reaching out to a few brokers.

With his experience in workforce management, labor relations, and operational know-how, he decided to target service-based local businesses—such as headhunting, recruiting, or temporary staffing agencies—rather than physical labor.

The first business he inquired about was a staffing company in Huntington Beach, listed for $750,000. But the books revealed unclear financial transactions between the corporation and the owner, and the staff didn't seem cheerful. Taejun didn't feel confident about the deal.

A few weeks later, a broker introduced him to a mid-sized company located near Wilshire, close to UCLA. After reviewing the financials, ownership information, and employee roster, he found the company made about $1.3 million in sales, but the asking price was $950,000—too high for comfort.

Taejun considered putting 20% down and financing the rest through an SBA loan. However, the seller's loan broker demanded additional collateral—his house and even his life insurance policy.

Having built a career at a global corporation, Taejun now felt uneasy about how different the local business world was—its deals, its risks. The thought of having to put up his life insurance as collateral made him hesitate.

In the end, Taejun gave up on acquiring an existing company and decided to build one from scratch. He incorporated a new business, hired staff, placed ads in the newspaper, and threw himself into launching a new venture.

~ ~ ~

Three years passed.

Taejun let out a long sigh of relief and thought, *If I had bought that Wilshire company three years ago, I would've lost both my house and the business.*

The subprime mortgage crisis had triggered a global financial meltdown. Companies were freezing hires or closing their doors altogether. Who in their right mind would use a staffing agency to hire employees during a crisis like that?

Back when he had been considering the Wilshire company, his wife, Yujin, had been firmly against it. She told him, "Spending nearly a million dollars to acquire a service business with no tangible assets— and then using your life insurance as collateral on top of that? It's too risky."

Had Taejun bought that business, he would have lost everything—his assets, his capital—and been left with nothing but a shell of a company. He had narrowly escaped a disaster. Even his own staffing agency was now receiving zero client requests for hiring. It was time to seek a new direction.

~ ~ ~

Around that time, Taejun received an email from the LA Chamber of Commerce.

"As part of our match-making program, we are arranging meetings with Cosmart. Interested companies, please reply."

Taejun had no experience in the food industry. Still, he expressed his interest and that evening, went to a nearby Chinese supermarket with Yujin. As they browsed the aisles, a product caught his eye. It was made in Korea and priced very competitively.

Suddenly, he remembered that "rice crackers" had been one of the items on Cosmart's consultation list.

He bought a few bags, found the Korean factory's contact information on the back of the packaging, and made a call timed for Korean business hours. He began exploring production and supply possibilities.

~ ~ ~

The day of the Cosmart meeting arrived.

Taejun brought along his assistant, Michelle, to take meeting notes, while he led the conversation himself. His company was running a staffing service under a DBA, but in this meeting, he used only the corporation's formal name—thankfully, the buyer wouldn't know his background in staffing.

The Cosmart buyer was a young woman who didn't look a day over thirty. Taejun answered her questions sincerely and humbly, but avoided discussing his past experience at multinational corporations. He focused on building trust and emphasizing the reliability and feasibility of supplying the product.

"Mr. Kang, I like your product, and I will send you the vendor setup package shortly."

Taejun couldn't hide his excitement at those words. Cosmart was a national membership-based retail giant with over 600 stores across the U.S. Supplying them wasn't just about a contract. It meant recognition.

Taejun murmured to himself in disbelief. "I… I'm actually supplying to Cosmart…"

A new path seemed to be opening once again. Taejun thought, *There is always a path.*

He had no idea that this moment would become a major turning point in the second half of his life. Cosmart—just the name itself made his heart swell.

CHAPTER 23

THE FUTURE

Taejun's business had achieved remarkable growth over the past decade. Starting with food products at the forefront, his company now included import and export companies involved in commodities such as coffee, along with advertising, brand licensing, and staffing services, with branches in Seoul and Bangkok.

He operated proprietary food manufacturing facilities and partner factories in the United States, Korea, China, Thailand, Vietnam, the Philippines, and Japan.

At the start of his food business, Taejun decided to establish supply channels exclusively targeting the top-tier companies in the U.S. He chose only five major retailers—Wallmax, Summit Club, Cosmart, Value Mart, and Krogins.

Having worked at a leading multinational company, Taejun believed it was strategically advantageous to sell to only the top players. Even when entering business partnerships with factories in Southeast Asia, he only signed supply contracts with companies equipped with the highest-grade facilities and more than 20 to 30 years of manufacturing experience.

During the early days, when he had no prior experience in food distribution, Taejun was supplying products to Cosmart. As he began supplying the same products to Summit Club and Wallmax, he received a phone call one day from Cosmart's buyer.

"Mr. Kang, you've slapped my face! It's our baby, and you and I created it together."

At first, Taejun didn't understand why Rachel, the buyer from Cosmart, was upset.

The issue was that he had supplied the same product—with identical packaging and pricing—to Summit Club, a direct competitor. This product had been developed from the ground up with Rachel: the contents, packaging, design, and size were all created in collaboration with her.

Taejun hadn't realized just how sensitive major U.S. retailers were, even over a single product. At the very least, he should have changed the design, adjusted the package size, and set different pricing. But he had not been aware of even these basic distribution courtesies.

Eventually, Rachel gave him an ultimatum: she would stop purchasing the product within three months.

Taejun was devastated. He only later learned that buyers at major retail chains visit competitor stores every weekend and adjust pricing by even a penny come Monday morning. This painful experience taught Taejun that, regardless of a business's size, every detail must be reviewed and executed with precision.

Fortunately, he was still supplying other juice products to Cosmart, and this became a stepping stone for expansion into other distribution channels. As the food business became his primary focus, Taejun took pride in donating food to a nearby shelter for single mothers.

He also supported the local high school football team, contributing small donations and offering game-day support—acts of meaning he was proud to carry out.

Now that his core food import and distribution business was firmly established, he had secured a

200,000 sq. ft. logistics warehouse in Riverside, enabling him to supply the entire U.S. without issue. He was also planning to expand to Nashville to serve a growing list of clients in the central region.

Taejun had recently noticed a shift from branded products toward private-label development. With retailers like Wallmax and Value Mart requesting their own branded lines, he ordered the activation of OEM supply from factories in Thailand, Vietnam, the Philippines, and Korea.

Wallmax alone had submitted five product projects worth approximately $20 million, and stable revenue was expected over the next two to three years. Orders continued to increase for Korean products such as snacks, coconut water, coffee, dried mangoes, hot sauce, frozen foods, dumplings, and japchae.

Now, Taejun reflected on the road he's traveled.

"Life is about survival."

He had pushed through countless fierce winds to get to this point. As he considered the day he would eventually leave this world, Taejun pondered what kind of mark he would leave behind. This led him to think seriously about "brands."

Brands that carry my soul, he thought.

It would be wonderful if his descendants carried them on, but even if they didn't, the fact that products bearing names he had created would live on in the world—infused with his soul—was meaningful enough.

And so, Taejun made up his mind to create five brands. He had three grandsons and two granddaughters. He believed that even after their grandfather was gone, if these brands remained close to them, they would remember him, reflect on his life, and live righteously by overcoming hardships and adversity.

Digging a small well to leave for his descendants—he believed that was his duty as a grandfather.

"I have to plant the fruit trees now so that my grandchildren can enjoy them 30 years from now." That was Taejun's conviction.

CHAPTER 24

THE PANDEMIC

Fernando died. For the past 15, no, nearly 20 years, Fernando had come every Saturday or Sunday to mow the lawn at Taejun's house. He died from COVID-19.

One weekend, during the height of the pandemic, a high school–aged girl rang the doorbell at Taejun's house. Next to her stood a man. It was Fernando's daughter.

Fernando hadn't shown up for two weeks, and Taejun had called to check in. Someone had told him that Fernando had contracted COVID. And now, the daughter had come in person.

"He's my dad, and he died of COVID a week ago."

Tears welled up in her eyes.

"What?" Taejun shouted.

"He had surgery, but unfortunately, he couldn't recover."

The man beside her, Fernando's brother, asked if he could continue mowing the lawn in his place. Later, Taejun heard that Fernando had life insurance, so his family wasn't immediately in financial danger. They said they planned to return to Mexico after the two daughters finished college.

A wave of sorrow washed over Taejun. Fernando had been a good man.

Years ago, Taejun had contacted the city about a beehive near his home, worried it might harm the children. But the city only removed hives attached to public buildings, not private homes. A pest control company quoted over $350 for three hours of work. So Taejun asked Fernando for help.

"Mr. Kang, I can't kill live animals."

What was he saying? He couldn't kill bees? He was the kind of man who hummed as he worked, cheerfully mowing the lawn.

~ ~ ~

News of death echoed across the world as the pandemic raged. People locked their doors tightly, paralyzed by fear. It felt like the end of the world.

Already, five or six people close to Taejun had passed away. Ann, the elderly woman across the street with diabetes, died of complications. Anthony's mother-in-law, who lived in a rental house, had fallen in the bathtub and broken her arm.

She was hospitalized and then contracted COVID. She passed away within two weeks.

Funerals had become a thing of the past. Even family members were not allowed at the burial. Every hour, the news updated the death toll in California and the number of hospitalizations, fueling the public's fear. Taejun felt this was the greatest crisis of his lifetime. He thought hard about how to survive.

First, he ordered all employees and factories to work remotely. He brought in a sanitation company to thoroughly disinfect the office and arranged for just one or two essential staff members to alternate shifts on-site.

More than business, Taejun valued the lives of his employees and their families. He closely monitored the situation, waiting to see how government policies would unfold.

Container shipping costs soared. At Long Beach Port, congestion delayed cargo unloading by weeks. Twenty to thirty container ships floated offshore, waiting to unload. Raw material prices were rising, and supply was unstable. Factories had to reduce production, while labor costs kept climbing.

In this emergency, Taejun didn't cling to old methods. He quickly adapted to the online market, conducted virtual meetings with buyers via Zoom, and encouraged his staff to explore new markets and secure alternative suppliers.

As the pandemic peaked and slowly began to decline, Taejun expanded supply through negotiations with major distributors, seeking new sales opportunities. His food business weathered the storm. To supply additional items, he began working with new factories in Thailand, the Philippines, Vietnam, and Korea. Except for frozen foods, container prices were gradually stabilizing.

"I survived another crisis," Taejun whispered to himself. "I made it through once again."

~ ~ ~

"What is life?"

Taejun fell deep into thought.

~ ~ ~

For the past 43 years, Taejun had a secret place where he went to find comfort. When life felt hopeless and he wanted to cry. When everything seemed to collapse and he felt like giving up. When joy overflowed and he had something to celebrate, he went to the same place: the view of the Long Beach shore and the Queen Mary from Hotel Serena.

Once called the Hilton, this beachfront hotel had a small café. He visited the place on special days. His favorite spot was by the window in a corner of the café. From that seat, he could see half of the Queen Mary Hotel. Though the ship never moved, it always looked as if it were departing just like him in the past.

He always ordered the same thing. A hot cup of coffee and a scoop of vanilla ice cream. The coffee woke up his body. The ice cream soothed his soul.

"This is enough," he would say to himself quietly, spooning the ice cream slowly.

That cold, sweet taste, blended with the bitterness of the years he had endured, offered him a moment of small, quiet peace when he made a lot of money, when deals fell through, and even on days he didn't want to talk to anyone.

At some point, the ice cream had become a kind of ritual. A small, gentle reward for surviving hard times. In that moment, he was not someone's husband, not someone's father, and not a company president. He was just a living man and a man who had survived.

CHAPTER 25

TOWARD THE SUN

Early in the morning, Taejun finished his breakfast with half a bagel and coffee made by Yujin, then got into the Uber he'd been waiting for.

At 10:15 a.m., he was flying to Bentonville on American Airlines flight AA4894 for an important meeting with Wallmax. Believing this would be a pivotal negotiation, he didn't delegate the task to a manager or team lead. He planned the trip himself to meet the buyer directly and make crucial decisions on the spot.

This meeting was for a large-scale project under the buyer's private label OEM brand, with the potential for long-term supply over several years. Even if it didn't reach all 4,000 stores, Taejun anticipated that at least 3,000 stores would carry their brand's products.

Taejun was always keeping pace with technology. For the past seven to eight months, he had actively implemented AI across all sectors of the company. From market analysis, product competitiveness reviews, new product planning, overseas manufacturer searches, competitor product and pricing analysis, marketing strategies, and even legal analysis, he was applying AI.

Back in the early 1990s, before the internet became mainstream, Taejun had already worked in internet-related departments in large corporations. He had deep insights and knowledge of the digital industry. He had even secured a domain in his own name more than 30 years ago.

His foresight and vision for the future still surpassed most.

~ ~ ~

The airport was chaotic and crowded with passengers heading east during the morning rush. Taejun got out of the Uber at the American Airlines terminal and stepped inside. He took the escalator toward security. He pulled out his laptop and placed it in a plastic bin, then put his shoes, belt, wallet, and all belongings in the tray. His backpack and small luggage went onto the conveyor belt.

Having passed through security, he put his shoes back on, gathered his belongings, and walked to a nearby Starbucks near the gate. He ordered a black Americano, took it to a window seat in a quiet, empty gate area, and took a sip.

Memories began to surface. Taejun smiled quietly.

About 43 years ago, I arrived in the U.S. at this very airport in L.A. with a daughter not yet two years old and a wife who knew nothing about America. All I had in my pocket was 183 dollars.

What kind of guts…It's almost laughable. Wasn't it as reckless as Don Quixote's charge?

A faint shimmer crossed Taejun's eyes. He wondered, *How on earth did I survive all those waves and storms, crossing mountains and rivers to make it here?*

It was a miracle.

Even Taejun had never considered himself a strong person. He simply enjoyed music and found peace sitting at a beach café, gazing at the ocean.

"What made me strong?" He searched within himself for the answer.

"It was the wind that blew against me. Sometimes, it came with storms. Sometimes, it was a tornado that swept everything away. But sometimes, it was a gentle spring breeze—warm and comforting."

While he had briefly lost himself in thought, the clock now read 9:30. A message alert sounded on his iPhone. Taejun quietly pulled out his work phone from his pocket. There was a message from his assistant, Michelle.

"Mr. Kang, we got some interesting news for you."

Taejun called her. There was a note of excitement in Michelle's voice. "Mr. Kang, I just got off the phone with a studio. They said your story might be something they'd like to explore further."

Taejun said nothing for a moment. Three or four months ago, he had felt the urge to organize the past 43 years of his life. Not to tell a glamorous story, but simply to leave behind the record of a life full of failures, comebacks, and constant challenges for his son, daughter, and grandchildren, and for someone else, still walking through a dark tunnel. So, every night, he quietly sat down in front of his laptop and began to write.

He had no expectations. Just a quiet hope that someone might appreciate that such a path existed. But after the book was published, unexpected emails and messages began to arrive.

"Your story gave me the courage to live again."

"I've been through something similar. It brought me to tears."

And today, a call came from a studio. Taejun smiled gently. At that moment, his story was no longer just his own.

When he approached the gate, boarding had just begun. As a first-class passenger, he boarded early and took a window seat. The flight attendant handed him a warm towel.

Looking out the airplane window, scenes from the past flashed before his eyes. For example, the health scare on a flight back from Montreal. Also, the time the right engine caught fire en route from New York to London, forcing an emergency landing.

Taejun stowed his luggage in the overhead bin and placed his backpack at his feet to access his laptop. That's when he noticed his shoes. He smiled again. He'd worn these shoes for nearly 20 years, having resoled them several times.

There were also long-associated items. Among them, a suit worn for over 20 years and a diary used for 35 years. Inside that diary is a faded currency exchange receipt—$183 from Narita Airport 43 years ago. He can't throw them away. They were his companions through hardship.

"All old things… but they carry history," he murmured to himself.

The plane took off. It's time to go again. Time to win again. This is the beginning of the fourth quarter.

"Like a gladiator, I must return with the bloody head of victory, dripping red."

Taejun's journey is never-ending. He runs toward the wind-blown hill.

CHAPTER 26

HOMECOMING

"It's time to leave." The sentence was written on a slip of paper. He folded it slowly, placed it in the desk drawer, and closed it quietly. Strangely, his heart was calm. There was nothing left to prove, nothing left to hold on to.

He felt the rest of his life could drift gently by amid the familiar winds and the scent of earth he had longed for. Nearly fifty years in America.

What he had built, what had crumbled, and what he had rebuilt—all passed before his eyes.

Success and failure, friends and foes, loves that were long and those that were brief.

None of it held him anymore.

~ ~ ~

Korean Air Flight KE018, departing LAX at 12:30 PM.

The California winter sky stretched clear beyond the window, but his gaze lingered somewhere beyond the blurred glass. As the plane glided down the runway, he closed his eyes.

"Incheon, 5:30 PM."

Once, numbers and timetables had defined his world. Now, only one word held meaning—arrival.

~ ~ ~

The cabin was quiet. He knew this was the final journey of his life. No more meetings, no more contracts, no more proving anything. In his bag were a thin coat, an old passport, and a single envelope. "258 Osan-ri, Haerim-myeon, Seosan-si, Chungnam."

It was the home where he had lived until he was eight; his uncle's house, now empty.

Neat, quiet, and ready to be lived in again with just a few belongings, he was about to begin life anew there.

~ ~ ~

A few days later, he headed for Seosan. Winter light soaked into the still plains of Chungcheong, and the village roads of Osan-ri, Haerim-myeon remained much as he remembered them.

The mountain behind the village still curled around it like a wide horseshoe and the old tile-roofed house nestled deep within still stood firm. It was the house where he was born and the place where his grandparents, father, siblings, and cousins had once lived together.

Though his grandparents had long passed, their presence lingered in every corner. The roof tiles had grown a little crooked with time, but remained strong. The wooden floor of the main room was warm in the sunlight. It was a house that would breathe again with a little care.

And he made a quiet promise to himself: "I'll fix this place. So my grandchildren can visit and play here."

~ ~ ~

Now, he begins a new life in his uncle's home at 258 Osan-ri, where he had once spent his childhood. The stone wall, the persimmon tree, even the yard where he once rode his bicycle were all still there.

Now, just one quiet soul in a countryside village, he would open the door each morning without a sound and greet the neighbors with gentle words.

~   ~   ~

A short distance away stood the family burial site—a tidy resting place passed down since his great-great-grandfather's time. It looked just as it had 20 years ago when he last visited.

The pine trees are carefully trimmed, a low stone wall quietly embracing the graves.

He knelt, folded his hands, and said, "Harabeoji, Halmoni... I've come. I'm a little late."

A breeze passed—low, quiet, and warm.

~   ~   ~

Beneath a stone beside the graves, he buried the envelope he had brought.

Inside was a simple will—a wish to be buried here as well.

~   ~   ~

Even the tiger returns to its cave when the journey nears its end. He too had come back—quietly, instinctively, without ceremony.

Not to conquer. Not to build. But simply to rest where it all began.

That night, he lay down in the small room at 258 and turned off the light. The ridgeline behind the village wrapped it in stillness beneath the night sky. The dim lights of a few homes flickered in the distance, and the world seemed to breathe in silent peace.

"I've returned." He whispered it in his heart.

~   ~   ~

Perhaps, if he wandered to Haemi-eupseong, he might run into his old elementary school classmates—the ones who once ran beside him, calling out his name.

Time may have passed, but surely—one day—they would meet again.

~ ~ ~

He had returned to his roots. And on that path, the wind no longer blew.

AFTERWORD

Writing this book has been a deeply personal journey. It reflects not only the fictional life of an immigrant who faced the winds of hardship and history but also echoes the countless real lives that have endured similar storms — including my own.

This story is inspired by years of observation, memory, faith, and reflection. Though Taejun's journey is fictional, his resilience and struggles are universal. I hope his path resonates with all those who have left something behind in pursuit of something greater.

I am grateful for the opportunity to share this story with you. It is my hope that readers — whether immigrants, dreamers, or wanderers — will find courage in Taejun's tears, and hope in his glory.

Thank you for walking this road with him, and with me.

Paul Han

Summer 2025

ABOUT THE AUTHOR

Paul Han

Paul Han is a Korean-American author, storyteller, and media producer whose body of work spans three central genres: inspirational Christian fiction, immigrant and business dramas, and emotionally rich romance novels.

With a deep foundation in faith and a lifelong commitment to writing, Paul's stories are known for weaving personal hardship, redemption, and hope into narratives that resonate across cultures and generations. His inspirational works — including *Faith Is Walking with God, Pray for Strong Demand,*

In the Wilderness, and *It's Not Over Yet* — reflect his journey of spiritual perseverance and are beloved by readers seeking comfort and strength through grace, prayer, and God's timing.

Paul also brings decades of international business leadership into his immigrant and corporate novels, such as the *Courage, Tears, and The Glory – The Immigrant Who Defied the Wind.* These works offer a rare and intimate look at the trials and triumphs of those who navigate foreign lands and boardrooms with dreams and scars alike.

As a multimedia creator, Paul integrates music and film into his storytelling. His internationally acclaimed romance novella *Unforgettable, My Love – Ayako* was released in English, Korean, and Japanese, reaching #1 in Literature & Fiction (Japanese) on Amazon. The story was accompanied by an original OST release and is part of a growing multimedia portfolio including YouTube read-alouds, theme songs, and audiobooks.

With multilingual publishing across Amazon (eBooks, paperbacks, hardcovers, and audiobooks), original music distributed via Distro-Kid, and emotional video storytelling on YouTube, Paul Han continues to build a cross-genre, cross-media literary world that uplifts, heals, and inspires.

Whether writing about lost love, spiritual resilience, or the immigrant pursuit of dignity, Paul's stories offer a singular message:

"No matter how far you fall — it's not over yet."